House of Durand 2

wanted by the vampires

ERIN BEDFORD

ALSO BY ERIN BEDFORD

<u>The Underground Series</u>
Chasing Rabbits
Chasing Cats
Chasing Princes
Chasing Shadows
Chasing Hearts
The Crimes of Alice

<u>The Mary Wiles Chronicles</u>
Marked by Hell
Bound by Hell
Deceived by Hell
Tempted by Hell

<u>Starcrossed Dragons</u>
Riding Lightning
Grinding Frost
Swallowing Fire
Pounding Earth

<u>The Celestial War Chronicles</u>
Song of Blood and Fire

<u>The Crimson Fold</u>
Until Midnight
Until Dawn
Until Sunset
Until Twilight

<u>**Curse of the Fairy Tales**</u>
Rapunzel Untamed
Rapunzel Unveiled

<u>**Her Angels**</u>
Heaven's Embrace
Heaven's A Beach
Heaven's Most Wanted

<u>**House of Durand**</u>
Indebted to the Vampires
Wanted by the Vampires

<u>**Academy of Witches**</u>
Witching On A Star
As You Witch
Witch You Were Here
Just Witch It

Granting Her Wish
Vampire CEO

House of Durand 2

wanted by the vampires

ERIN BEDFORD

CHAPTER 1
Marcus

"I UNDERSTAND YOUR CONCERN, Marcus, but we cannot just let Valentine back us into a corner." Antoine's voice held all the exasperation he felt about the subject. It wasn't surprising since I'd hounded him about it every day for the last week.

Antoine's office was as meticulous as ever. Every book was in its place, every paper where it belonged. There wasn't even a single paper clip left astray. Sometimes I wondered why our esteemed leader even needed a maid in the first place.

I'd been against getting a live-in maid from the beginning. A cleaning service would have worked just as well with fewer complications. However, the rest of my brothers had a need to have someone pick up after them. Perhaps part of it was my brothers wanted someone to bother or dote on depending on their whim.

That desire brought us to our current subject, Piper Billings. A simple name for a more than complicated woman. She had weaseled her way into our house and into the hearts of at least two of my brothers... or so it seemed. Antoine and the twins were harder to read than Rayne and Wynn. Those two were easier to read than anyone, even though they tried to cover it up in their own special way, Rayne with anger and Wynn with a flippant attitude. Someone who didn't know them wouldn't have been able to see it, but as we'd been together for several decades, not much slipped past me.

Except for Antoine.

Our leader and savior was more than an expert on hiding his true feelings and intentions. I had to work extra hard to get a read on him, like I was trying to do now.

"Valentine will not stop until we get rid of her or give her to him." I crossed my large arms over my chest, my gaze set on the man before me. "If you won't give him to her, then you need to eliminate the cause of his attraction."

Sighing, Antoine sat his pen down and locked those icy blue eyes on me. "Even if I dismissed Miss Billings, there is no guarantee that Valentine won't go looking for her on his own." He pushed his shoulders back and his braided blonde hair fell over his shoulder. "No, she is better kept where we can keep an eye on her."

"Then at least bind her."

"No."

That one word resonated through the room and told me that I'd already pressed my luck. I could keep pushing him, but it would not have a pleasant outcome. I'd been on the receiving end of Antoine's wrath a time or two in our long life together, and it was not something I enjoyed.

No, better to let it lie and try again later. Perhaps if I were able to convince the others to let her go, then Antoine would be more willing to comply.

With a jerk of my head, I turned on my heel and left his office. I'd always prided myself on being a man of few words. There was a time to speak up and a time to stay silent. Right now, it was the former.

I walked toward the library where I knew one of my brothers, Wynn, would be lounging about. It was already past midnight, and most places in town would be closed. There wasn't much a vampire could do after nightfall here. The bars closed at one, and unless you were looking for a pharmacy, there wasn't much nightlife. While that was something I enjoyed about this town, my other brothers were frustrated by it.

Wynn, for instance, loved the attention of the mortals. He had voted for our house to live in some place 'fun.' at least in his eyes. New York or Los Angeles, those were his top picks. Living in the middle of Georgia in a town that barely had a library and a movie theater wasn't his idea of fun.

But he was young, younger than Antoine and me. We long since had gotten over the need to be in the middle of it all. The pheromones humans gave off would fill the clubs and parties like a thick fog which vampires would revel in. We enjoyed blood the most, of course, but knowing what humans wanted was just as filling.

It wasn't the same as mind reading, not like Rayne, who could see right inside your mind as if he were watching one of those television sets. It took time and practice to build enough of a wall up to keep him out. It was exhausting, and most of us didn't bother anymore.

When I pushed open the heavy door of the library, I was so lost in thought that I didn't notice our little maid trying to leave. With a small oomph and a bump against my chest that I barely felt; Piper fell toward the hardwood floor. My hand automatically shot out and caught her wrist to stop her descent mid-fall.

"Oh, shit." She gasped, her chestnut colored eyes darting from side to side as she tried to regain her bearings.

With a little tug, I pulled her to her feet only inches from myself. Against my better judgment, I inhaled deeply. The scent of her filled my senses, and I felt myself harden. Peculiar that a woman like her with her big doe eyes and heart-shaped face could cause such a reaction in me. I hadn't felt that kind of immediate arousal in years... if ever.

"Thank you," Piper murmured, her eyes darting down to the floor as she shifted in place. "I should have been watching where I was going."

"I ran into you."

The rumble of my voice seemed to startle her, and her eyes widened, her head jerking up to meet my gaze. I cocked my head to the side, to search for what was so attractive about her that she had us all falling over ourselves to keep her.

Well, almost all of us.

"Still, I should have been paying attention. I get used to being by myself during the day I forget you guys live here too." She huffed a laugh, tucking a hair behind her ear and showing off her dangling silver earrings. Three tiny crosses attached with small circles between them swung in the air and bumped against her jawline.

"Those don't work," I told her with a nod of my head.

Her brows furrowed, and she pulled back slightly, then her hand reached up and touched the dangling crosses. "Oh." The small word made her lips form into a perfect O-shape before her brows shot up to her forehead as she shook her head back and forth. "No, no. I would never... I mean, I didn't pick them because you're vampires." Piper continued to ramble on and muttered apologies, her heart beating rapidly as I stared down at her.

"Marcus. Enough."

Piper quieted, and her head jerked toward the voice. Wynn approached, his hands in his pockets and a languid sort of movement to his gait. His black hair curled as it brushed his shoulders, and his eyes bright blue twinkled with mirth. I could see his tattoo of our house sigil between the folds of his unbuttoned shirt, the same one that matched the one above my heart.

"Wynn, when did you get here?" Piper's voice became low and breathy, her heart skipping a beat as she looked dreamily at Wynn.

Interesting.

"I've been here the entire time." Wynn gave her one of his trademark smiles, the smile that usually had women dropping their pants for him in seconds. He pointed a finger at Piper and wiggled it around. "You should pay more attention to your surroundings. Isn't it past your bedtime?"

Piper's cheeks turned an interesting color of pink, and she ducked her head before giggling. "I couldn't sleep. I was looking for something to read." She held up the books in her hands, and my eyes finally dipped below her face.

The short, silky shorts and the tank top that hugged her curvy frame collaborated with her story. My eyes briefly registered how she hadn't put a bra on beneath her top and how the cool library had made that fact quite prominent.

Wynn clearly noticed as well. His tongue slid across his top teeth, and he bared his fangs to her for a brief second before turning his eyes from the tempting maid to me. "Were you looking for me, brother?"

I inclined my head in a nod.

"Then, by all means, let's head to the kitchen. I could use a drink." He gave Piper a sideways glance that made me think he was contemplating taking a bite out of her. That was strictly against the rules... not that Wynn ever had intentions of following any of Antoine's rules.

"You should go to bed, it's not safe in these halls after dark." Wynn winked, and that made her giggle once more. It was a pretty sound, one that I wouldn't mind hearing more of. I could understand why they would all want to keep her around.

But what we wanted and what was needed wasn't the same thing.

"Yes, brother." I opened the door and gestured outside into the hallway. "Let us drink."

CHAPTER 2
Piper

BLEACH BURNED MY NOSE as I scrubbed at the bathtub in Allister's bathroom. It made my eyes tear up and my nose itch. My fingers were going numb from scrubbing so much, but either Allister was fucking with me or he had killed a whole lot of something.

I was hoping for the former. No one wanted to be cleaning blood regularly, but thinking back to the beginning of this job, I realized that was exactly what I'd been doing.

"Fucking psychos," I muttered to myself as I shook my head.

One would think that after weeks of cleaning this house that I would get used to the nuances that came with working for the Durand brothers. Well, I guess they weren't brothers in the traditional, related-by-blood way. I still wasn't quite sure how that all worked. They weren't exactly throwing out answers like candy around here.

Since my revelation about the vampiric nature of my bosses or, ick, masters, as they wanted to be called, life has been relatively normal... if you ignored the dinner party with the slutty vampirina and creepy Valentine. They made horror movies about guys like him.

Ever since I'd gotten those flowers from my new undead admirer, I'd had nightmares that kept me up at night, so much so that I ended up having to find the most boring books in the library just to knock me out. Last night's run-in with Marcus and Wynn made me flush in embarrassment.

When I slipped out of my bedroom, I'd never expected to run into anyone, or I would have put something else on. It wasn't until I was in the chilly library with two of brothers that I realized how little I had been wearing.

If Marcus noticed, he didn't show it, but Wynn clearly did.

Remembering the hungry look in Wynn's sapphire blue eyes, I shivered. We hadn't had many run-ins since Valentine and Theresa had visited. I'd done my best to avoid all of them the best I could, especially Wynn.

Even if I hadn't already been panty-dropping crazy about him before I took his blood to heal my wrist that Rayne 'accidently' broke, I couldn't be around him now without wanting to jump him. It was an obvious side effect of taking his blood. However, I noticed that the more days that passed, the less aggressive the hold was on me. Sure, I still wanted to tear Wynn's clothes off and have my wicked way with him, but it was more on a normal human level now and less 'I'm being forced to want you.'

With that thought in my head, I finished up cleaning Allister's bathroom, something I was going to get back at him in some way for later, and headed to the next room on my list, Rayne's.

While Valentine and Wynn were still important issues, they didn't trump the biggest one I had, Rayne. Loud-mouthed, too sexy for his own good, and a major pain in my ass.

Ever since he kissed me to save me from Valentine, I hadn't been able to shake these feelings for him. Well, the one feeling, a singular feeling that made me want to jump his bones every time I saw him.

So, he was also on my list of masters to avoid. Which you think wouldn't be hard when we had an opposite sleep schedule, but I still ended up running into Rayne on occasion. Either on purpose, his, not mine, or because fate was having a laugh on my behalf.

It wasn't like I hated him. He was a pain, of course, but one damn fine kisser. The hero thing, saving me from Valentine, put a cherry on top of the already dangerous bad boy part of the whole vampire hottie package.

"I thought I might find you here," Rayne's voice came from behind me, stepping right out of my thoughts into reality.

I jolted, and pain exploded through my head as I hit it on the bathroom sink. Groaning and grabbing my head, I eased back onto my heels, sponge still in hand.

"Are you okay?" Rayne said as he appeared beside me, concern filling his features as his hand reached out as if he was going to touch me. He thought better of it and dropped the hand as he waited for me to answer.

"Don't sneak up on people, and you won't be responsible for causing them to mental issues," I told him with more snap than I wanted.

Hurt skated across his features, and those amber eyes flinched away from me for a split-second, but then it was gone. His face smoothed over, and in place of the hurt, there was an arrogant snarl.

"Well, maybe a hit or two on the head would make you a better person." He scowled and stood to his feet. "God knows your personality sucks as it is."

Jumping up after him, I threw the sponge down and shoved a finger at his face. He wasn't much taller than me, so it put us at an even level, something I was thankful for when trying to be threatening. "You listen here if anyone needs a personality adjustment it's you. You're an asshole and a jerk, and... and..."

Rayne grabbed my offending finger and jerked me closer until our bodies aligned with one another. I could make out the freckles on his pale skin and the different shades of red in his hair. The hot feel of his breath on my face made me ache in new ways than before.

"And totally hot for you," he murmured. His eyes locked with mine, and for a moment

I thought he was going to kiss me. Those long pale lashes of his fluttered as his face dipped down, but I pushed him away.

"Don't do that."

He released me with a confused frown. "Don't do what? Kiss you?"

"Yes." I pulled down my polo shirt and leaned down to pick up my discarded sponge. Giving him my back, I went about gathering the rest of my cleaning supplies. "I don't have time for whatever sick game you are playing."

"Who said I was playing?" Rayne came up behind me, his words a hot promise of something, something I couldn't let myself believe. I knew him. He was just as bad as Valentine.

There were two possible reasons why he was here now. One, he genuinely wanted me and was looking to pick up where things left off that night of the dinner party, or two, he just wanted to mess with me. Rayne could sense how much that kiss had affected me, and it's not like I could very well control my reaction to him now, anyway. So, the only conclusion was that he'd come to torture me about it.

"Stop thinking so much." Rayne placed a hand on my shoulder and spun me around.

"I'm not as much of a dick as you want me to be."

"Says you," I snapped and shifted away from him. I brushed past him and out of the bathroom, then made my way across Allister's bedroom toward the door. I could hear Rayne following me but wasn't going to give him the satisfaction of looking at him. "You know, just because Antoine pays me—"

"We."

"What?" I paused and peered back at him.

Rayne leaned against the bedpost of Allister's four poster bed and crossed his arms over his chest. He was shorter than his brothers but no less muscular. Still, he wasn't like a football player or one of those beefy guys who spent more time at the gym than at home. No, Rayne was more like a soccer player with lean muscle from running up and down a court all day.

"Soccer? Really?" Rayne cocked a brow at me.

Had I said that out loud? Must have. I grabbed the sponge from my bucket and threw it at him. To my dismay, he dodged it and appeared at my side in a flash.

"Leave me alone," I growled.

"Gladly," he leaned in close as if to tell me a secret, "but I want to make clear that Antoine doesn't just pay your salary. We all do. You aren't his maid. You're ours. So, I have as much a reason to torture you as the others."

I let out a frustrated growl. "Do you ever hear yourself talk? You sound like a complete and utter douchebag." A fucking fantastic kisser of a douchebag.

Rayne shifted back and smirked. "A fucking fantastic kisser douchebag," he said, even miming my inner voice as I had said it to myself.

I gaped at how he had literally just read my mind. It wasn't possible. I shook my head and spun on my heel, marching out of the room and into the hallway. The wooden floors gleamed where I had recently polished them, and a long maroon runner covered the middle of the hallway, making it seem like it was leading you to somewhere. However, that somewhere was the end of the hall where a single window covered in heavy drapes stood.

Pulling open one of the drapes, I positioned myself in the light of the morning sun. If anything, the sun would keep Rayne at a safe distance from me, and I needed a break, anyway. With a satisfied hum, I spun around to tell Rayne as much, but he hadn't followed me.

"Huh." I let out a sigh and tried to tell myself that it wasn't disappointment swirling in my gut. I stood in the sun a bit longer, expecting Rayne to pop out of nowhere at any moment, and then as the minutes ticked on, I realized he wasn't coming. I shook my head, picked up my things, and made my way to the next room.

As I was turning the doorknob to Drake's room, the sound of footsteps coming up the stairs reached me. I froze. Had Rayne waited for me to get out of the sun before making his grand reappearance? A part of me hoped he had because, if anything, fighting with him sure made my day less boring.

Sadly, it wasn't.

Darren appeared at the top of the stairs, dressed in his usual black slacks and suit jacket. his shirt had clearly been recently pressed along with his bow tie. He wore his ebony hair slicked back from his gorgeous face and a pair of white gloves. There was something so peculiar about how he dressed. It was so very butler-like that it was scary, as if he had stepped out of one of those television shows set in the nineteenth century. Really, who expected their workers to dress like that?

Then again, I had been expected to wear some Lolita maid outfit for the dinner party with Valentine so I couldn't say who got the short end of the stick there.

"Ah, there you are." Darren walked toward me, his shiny dress shoes making next to no sound on the wood floors. "I was hoping to catch you this morning."

"Uh, yeah." I shifted in place to face him fully. "I skipped breakfast and was working through your list of chores. Did you need something?"

Usually, Darren and I had a pretty professional relationship. He certainly tried to keep me at arm's length no matter how much I tried to be his friend. I tried not to take it personally. He was blood bound to Antoine, and I was an outsider. Who knew if I would one day leave, and we'd never see each other again? Based on how many maids they'd gone through, I could hardly blame him.

"Why don't we go to the kitchen and have a cup of coffee?" Darren offered with a small smile. I didn't trust that smile. He never wanted to have a coffee break with me. To ask me now was suspicious.

Too curious to say no, I shrugged. "Sure, I was just about to take a break, anyway."

"Wonderful." He clasped his hands and then swept one out and toward the stairs. "Shall we?"

I nodded, and as we walked side by side, the pleasantries dropped, and we settled into an awkward silence. Well, more for me than him. I didn't think Darren had an awkward bone in his body, or at least, he didn't show it. He was one hard man to read.

"So, what did you want to talk about?" I asked, trying to fill the quiet as we walked down the stairs.

"I'd prefer to speak in private rather than out here in the open." Darren gestured around us.

My eyes caught onto the large chandelier hooked to the middle of the ceiling in the foyer. I'd never get used to how beautiful this house was. Over twenty rooms, most closed off to save electricity and cleaning, thank God, several bathrooms, a large dining room, a drawing room, a huge library, and even a ballroom were only a few of the things about the house I enjoyed. Let's not forget about the fully stocked kitchen filled with the latest appliances and my own bedroom. It was much more than I was used to, that was for sure.

Before I'd come to work for the Durands, I'd been hopping from one clerical job to the other after my former company went under, leaving their employees jobless and without any promising prospects. I didn't know what my ex-coworkers had done. I hadn't been much of a socializer at the time.

But me, I had ended up having to give up my dog and my apartment to live out of my car. It was how I was living when I finally got the job here as the live-in maid, not that Darren was too happy with that development. He'd been dead set against me working here.

I didn't know why at the time, of course, but now, I could see he had a good reason.

The Durands were vampires. Fast, hungry, way too attractive for deadly killers, and with super hearing to boot.

"Why the kitchen? Why does it matter?" I angled my head to him with a curious arch of my brow. "Not like anything in this house is private. You should know that."

Frowning at my words, Darren continued to walk toward the kitchen. "They aren't all powerful. They do have their limits. The kitchen will suffice."

"Fine." I sighed and followed him down the hallway and past the door to the basement where I knew our masters of the house were sleeping. I wondered briefly if Rayne were down there, sleeping. Then I shoved it aside.

Don't think about him.

Once we went through the dining room and into the kitchen, Darren promptly went to the sink. He turned the water on and then went to the cabinet. He pulled down two cups and placed them on saucers before pouring the coffee. I sat the island in the middle of the kitchen, on one of the three bar stools and waited. He sat one in front of me and the other before him the opposite side of the island before bringing a small tray of sugar and cream between us as well as a plate of blueberry scones.

"You can talk freely now." He gestured to the water faucet still running. "They won't be able to hear us now." He pushed the plate of scones closer to me.

"Oh, bringing out the big guns now are ya?" I grinned at him before picking up one of the pastries. "You must really want something from me."

Darren let out an impatient huff as he poured cream into his cup and then added a single cube of sugar. It was strange that they had cubes. Really, who even made them that way anymore? Most people just used the powdered stuff and were done with it. I suppose they thought they were fancier this way.

Once he was done stirring his coffee, he picked it up and took a sip. Watching him was like watching some kind of alien life form. It was all so fascinating. From the way he held his cup like it was something that would break in his hands at any moment to the way his mouth covered the rim of the cup and drank from it without a sound.

"Stop looking at me that way," Darren demanded.

"What way?" I grinned back as I took a bite of my scone. Yum. Crumbly and tart. The cook, Gretchen, must have made these. No way they were store bought.

Darren scowled. "Like I'm some kind of science experiment."

"Sorry," I said through a full mouth. "You're just so... polished." He gave me an exasperated look that made me giggle. "What you are? No one in the real-world dresses like you or is half as sophisticated."

With a disgusted grunt, Darren set his gaze upon his cup. "Believe me, I know."

"So," I sat my scone down and brushed the crumbles from my hands before leaning my elbows on the kitchen island, "you've fed me and watered me. What do you want to talk about?"

Darren's lips pressed into a thin line for a moment as if he were trying to figure out how to word his question. Then after a solid minute, he asked, "Have you told anyone about the flowers?"

My hand froze in mid-lift of my coffee cup. After the dinner party and Rayne's heroic rescue, Valentine had requested to buy me from Antoine, something that appalled me even now the moment I thought of it. Who treated people like cattle or inanimate objects? I was a human being, not a thing.

Thankfully, Antoine had refused him, but that hadn't stopped Valentine from trying. He had sent me flowers every day for the last week since he left, each time with a creepier message than before. 'See you soon.' 'Can't wait to see your smiling face.' 'Your blood smells of the finest wines. I can't wait to taste it.' On and on they went, each day a different kind of flower, like he was trying to woo me in some sick twisted way.

At the mention of the flowers, I glanced around the kitchen. When I didn't see a vase of them waiting for me, I sagged and released a stuttering breath. I turned my attention back to Darren.

"No, I haven't," I answered at last. "I don't see the point. Antoine told him no. What do a few flowers mean?"

Darren shook his head. "Master Durand might have told Valentine no, but clearly he hasn't stopped trying to pursue you. The flowers are his way of making you remember. That he isn't going to give up, and while we're on the topic of keeping secrets..." Darren locked eyes with me and stared with such intensity that I was worried I'd done something. I quickly searched my mind for anything I might have broken recently.

Nope. Nothing.

"You should watch your thoughts around Rayne," the butler finished.

My eyes widened. "Uh, Rayne. What about Rayne? Why should I watch myself around Rayne?" Why the hell couldn't I stop saying his name? Rayne. Fuck.

Darren gave me an impatient look and tilted his head to the side. "I'm going to pretend like there is nothing there to worry about. However, I think it is the right time to tell you about the masters'... abilities."

"Uh, abilities?" My brows furrowed. "I already know about that stuff. They're vampires." I lifted my hand and ticked off what I knew. "Fast. Hot. Super hearing. No sunlight. Likes blood. What else is there to know?"

Clearing his throat, Darren nodded. "While those are all true, they have other abilities as well."

"Like what? Changing into bats?" My eyes lit up, and I wiggled in my seat. "Oh, can they poof into smoke like Dracula?"

Letting out an impatient sigh, Darren held a hand up. "No."

"Then what are they?" I leaned forward on my elbows, eager to hear the rest. "Come on, don't hold out on me now."

"I cannot divulge to you all of our masters' secrets," Darren began with a frown. "However, I do believe it is prudent for you to know that Master Rayne's ability allows him to do more than the others in terms of... privacy."

"What do you mean?" I cocked my head to the side and then laughed nervously. "He doesn't have x-ray vision, does he?" When Darren didn't immediately deny it, I gaped and covered my chest feeling violated. "He has x-ray vision! What the hell? Of all the perverted—"

Darren sighed. "Calm yourself. He cannot see through your clothing. However, he can see into your mind."

My mouth fell open. I couldn't find my words or my breath. I kept making a sound like a wheezing walrus that had me holding tightly onto the counter for dear life.

Oh my God. Rayne could read my mind. Rayne *could read my mind!*

I felt so violated, even more so than if he had been able to see through my clothing. One's mind was a personal place. A safe haven to say all the bad things you never would say out loud, and to have that intruded upon by someone without you knowing? Why, that was just... just...

"It's wrong, that's what it is." I slammed my hand down on the counter, my jaw clenched tight. "Why didn't you tell me before?"

Darren lifted a shoulder. "It was not important. We weren't sure if we could trust you, and now that we do, I find it important that you watch what you think around Master Rayne, especially if you would like to keep the Valentine incident to yourself."

"Well, thank you for letting me know. I'll be sure to adjust accordingly." Meaning I'd be giving Rayne an earful and then some next time I saw him. "As for Valentine, well, I haven't responded to any of his notes, and I don't plan to." I drank deeply from my coffee cup to give my rapidly beating heart a moment to calm down. "He'll get bored, eventually."

"Pfft." Darren turned away from the island with his cup, having finished his coffee already. "You clearly don't know vampires."

"Obviously not. Why don't you enlighten me?" I watched him with impatient curiosity. They were just flowers. It wasn't like he was peeping through my window or leaving disturbing messages on my phone. Sure, the guy was a creep, but I could imagine worse stalkers.

"Vampires are predators," Darren started as he washed his cup and placed it in the drainer. "They live for the hunt. The more you deny them, the more they will want to catch you. Never mind that you have never responded to him." Darren turned and faced me as he wiped his hands on a dish towel. "He will see your non-response as a reason to keep trying, and he will. He will get tired of the flowers eventually, of course. However, what he does next might be worse, and you will be begging for the day that all you had to worry about was a dozen posies and a disturbing note."

He tossed the dish towel onto the counter and marched out of the kitchen. I sat there alone, lost in thought until my coffee went cold and a sour taste formed in my mouth. With a sinking suspicion, I stood from the island and walked over to the trash can. With a deep breath, I lifted the lid. Inside were pink posies and a note signed with a V. I didn't read the note but closed the lid and

stalked out of the kitchen, not bothering with
the mess I'd left behind.

CHAPTER 3
Rayne

MY EARS STRAINED TO hear what Piper and Darren were talking about, but the damn butler had been around us too long. All I could hear was water running.

"Fuck," I growled and shifted on my bed. I shoved my fingers into my pillow, trying to make it more comfortable so that I could sleep, but that sweet release was far from my reach.

The basement where my brothers and I spent our days sleeping was almost as big as the mansion above it. Six twin beds were lined up the wood paneled walls. That wood covered up the cold concrete that made up the basement, like the wooden floors hid the hideous cold floors. Not that the cold would have bothered any of us. Temperatures didn't really register when you're dead.

Correction, undead.

As well as the well-appointed sleeping quarters, we had a fully stocked fridge filled with blood and any other snacks we might be craving. Add that to the flat screen T.V. and the bathroom we had to share, and it was the perfect hideaway for any modern vampire. There was no reason to leave or go upstairs to the main house, not if we didn't want to.

Except it didn't have one thing.

Piper.

Sweet, sexy, smart-mouthed Piper Billings.

That mouthy maid had wormed her way into our house and our lives. Not one of us in the family hadn't been affected by her. Even Marcus with all his silent brooding couldn't resist her.

"What's got you in a mood?" Wynn tossed a book at my bed, and I jolted up and caught it before it hit me. With a smug grin, he lounged back on his bed, shirtless and flipping the pages of another book sitting in his lap at leisure. I wasn't even sure if he was reading it.

"Nothing, just tired." I put the book on the nightstand next to me rather than throwing it back.

Wynn noticed. He cocked his head to the side, and his black hair fell over his face. Those icy blue eyes of his bored into me and made me even more annoyed. It was almost like he could read my mind which was impossible.

"Something happened, didn't it?" He threw his legs over the side of the bed and leaned toward me with a fang-toothed grin. "With Piper."

"What happened with Piper?" Drake asked, glancing over his shoulder from where he and his twin, Allister sat on the couch. They were playing the latest video game, something about hunting vampires. Ironic.

With hair a dark brown one shade away from being black, the twins were big men with more muscle then should be possible without going to the gym every day. They were a perfect match, almost down to the dimples in their cheeks. Even their abilities complimented each other, Drake with his stronger than usual sexual allure and Allister with his silver tongue. He could probably talk the Pope into committing mass murder. Together, they would have been unstoppable.

Well, if they weren't living the quiet life in the middle of Georgia.

"Nothing happened," I tried to reassure them so they'd leave me alone, but I should have known better. The more I denied it, the more they would probe me.

"Just tell me that it wasn't something the little human isn't going to bitch about to me tomorrow?" Antoine demanded from his desk in the corner. He was still working. Hell, he was always working.

They were all down here with me tonight, a rare occurrence. Usually, at least Antoine was upstairs doing paperwork or taking calls he couldn't take after hours. If I weren't so irritated, I'd think it was nice to have their company.

"No, it was nothing." I walked to the fridge and pulled out a container of blood. Only Gretchen was allowed down here to refill the fridge. Even Piper had to stay upstairs, so it was up to us to keep the place relatively clean. No one wanted to live in a pig sty.

"But something did happen." Wynn appeared next to me in a flash and grabbed his container of blood before I could close the door to the fridge.

I shook my head and begged that they would let it go.

"It's alright, we all find Piper interesting. You wouldn't be the first to lose your head over a human." Wynn wagged his brows suggestively.

Wynn wanted anyone with a heartbeat and tits, so it wasn't surprising he wanted Piper. She obviously wanted him too. I didn't need to be a mind reader to figure that out. The twins, too, had a weird fascination with her. It wasn't quite adoration, more like the interest you'd have for a child or pet. It wasn't quite attraction either, but they couldn't stop messing with her either.

Now, Antoine was something else.

I always had a hard time getting a good read on him. It might be because he was so much older than the rest of us, or he was just good at blocking his mind from me. Either way, I couldn't tell if he even cared if Piper lived or died. Not that I hadn't tried to find out.

Thankfully, Marcus was the only one of us who didn't care one way or the other about the maid. Sure, he noticed her, but if he had any feelings for her, he has kept them firmly in check and out of his mind. He sat on his bed with his eyes closed but ears open as usual, listening but not engaging in the conversation.

I sat down on the edge of my bed and took a long drink of the blood. With a sigh, I confessed, "She's been avoiding me."

Allister laughed. "Well, can you blame her?"

"You're a dick to her the whole time she's here," Drake pointed out before pausing his game. He and Allister turned around in near-perfect unison and threw an arm a piece over the back of the couch as they faced me.

"Then you played the hero and saved her from Valentine," Allister continued with a mocking grin.

Drake made a kissing face before chuckling. "And not only did you steal a kiss, but you got a taste of that delicious blood of hers." The twins both closed their eyes and hummed as if they tasted it for themselves. Drake opened his eyes first and looked at me. "Who knew it would be the least of us to get the first taste?"

I scowled and, without a word, picked up the book from my nightstand and threw it at his head. Unfortunately, Drake caught it between his hands and only laughed harder at my expense.

"Fuck off." I flopped back down on my bed and turned my back to them. I'd had enough of their teasing for the day.

"Language," Antoine warned from his desk. We were vampires, and all he cared about was if we were cursing. What a joke.

There was a shift in the air in the room as Marcus finally spoke. "I am less concerned about Rayne's adolescent habits and more concerned about what they are keeping from us."

"They who?" Drake asked.

"Piper and Darren," Wynn explained from somewhere near the twins. I had my back to them, but I could feel them moving around, their minds racing with different thoughts. Allister, the dumbass, was the only one not thinking about the two humans in the house. His mind was focused on his vampire killer video game and how he could get beat the next level.

Drake ignored his brother's need to play the game and stood from the couch. He moved across the room until he was on the other side of Antoine still sitting at his desk. "He's your blood servant. Aren't you worried?"

He was now in my line of sight, and I could see the tension in his large shoulders... and I could also see the sigil of our house tattooed over his chest through the thin, white tank top he wore.

I'd never thought about getting a tattoo before, certainly not before I became a vampire. However, when we finally had permission to leave our sire's home and make a house of our own, it was mandatory to solidify our bond and loyalty to the House of Durand. I hadn't regretted taking the mark, not a single day of my undead life since I'd been here and certainly not today.

"I am not as concerned as you are about my blood servant. Darren will confide in me when he believes it is worth my attention." Antoine calmly went back to writing on whatever he was working on. He always chose to write over using the computer. It was sort of strange, as if he were trying to separate himself from this century. I supposed there was something we all clung to from our past.

"They have been acting suspiciously for days," Drake tried again as he gestured to the room. "We've all noticed it. The tension in them, the way they stop talking when they think we are close. It's dangerous."

Antoine placed his pen down and turned in his chair to locking eyes with Drake. He didn't even have to speak or raise his voice to make the large man flinch, just that look.

With Drake cowed, Antoine crossed one long leg over the other and placed his hands on top of his knee.

"And what, pray tell, would you have me do?" he probed. "They are allowed their privacy. Should I force them to spill all their secrets to me? What about you? Do you have secrets that you wish to tell?"

"Of course, not but—"

"Then it is prudent to not require absolute honesty from our family members and staff, else we will find ourselves without either." Antoine's gaze softened. "Now, I trust Darren. He will do what he thinks is right until the time comes that he will need our assistance. I did not make him my blood servant simply for his pretty face."

Wynn snorted at that.

Antoine didn't move his head, but his next words were definitely directed at Wynn. "Speak, and I will remove your tongue. Let you spend the next week practicing your sign language."

Wynn had brains enough not to speak any further, and the tension in the room settled after a moment or two. Drake went back to the couch with Allister and began his video game once more, but now there were a few more curses and growls as they played.

Good for them. We all had to get our anger out some way or the other, and at least the twins had found a healthy outlet for it. They had their games. Meanwhile, Wynn screwed everything that walked, I painted, and Antoine buried himself in work. Marcus, well, no one really knew how Marcus dealt with his anger, if he even had any. Some days I thought he was more robot than vampire.

I wondered what Piper did to blow off steam.

I spent the rest of the day thinking up all the different things she might do before I finally drifted off into oblivion.

CHAPTER 4
Antoine

THERE IS A MOMENT in every vampire's long life in which he wishes to have never chosen immortality. This was one of them.

"I'm telling you, Mr. Durand, I triple checked the numbers. We're still missing over half a million dollars in that investment account," the quaky voice of my accountant, Joey, squeaked in my ear. He was a tiny blip of a man, not hardly worth the thousands I paid him to keep our household accounts up to date, but he accepted our odd hours and didn't ask too many questions.

However, this time, I knew he was lying to me.

"Are you sure, Joseph?" I calmly asked as I pushed my powers of persuasion into my voice.

Each vampire awakened to a certain type of power when they were changed. Some discovered the ability to levitate, some shapeshifting, and still, others didn't get anything. I happened to have been blessed or cursed, depending on how you viewed it, with multiple gifts. One of those gifts was the ability to force my will onto another. I didn't like to use my power if I didn't have to. Taking someone's choice away had never been my particular kink. I preferred people to come to me willingly rather than be forced. It made things so much more enjoyable.

However, Joey was not a smart man. He thought he was pulling the wool over the eyes of an old-fashioned client. As if I wouldn't notice the money was missing or question it. I could use a computer just like anyone else. I just preferred to use paper and pen over such bipolar machines. They hated me as much as I hated them.

"Y-yes?" Joey stuttered out, and I could feel him fighting my persuasive tone. "I think so, I mean, I'm sure. Yes. I'm sure. Someone must have taken it or moved it to another account? I can run the numbers and see where it might have—"

"That won't be necessary." I sighed and leaned back in my office chair. "I know exactly where the money has gone, and I expect every cent of it back where it belongs by the year-end. Am I understood?" This time I pushed my powers through the phone line even harder to make sure my commands stuck.

"Of course, of course. Mr. Durand, the money will be back there at the year's end. You can count on me. I will make it happen. I—"

"Good." I hung up the phone and tossed it on the top of my large office table. As I leaned my elbows on the table, I rubbed my temple. One would think that, as the undead or whatever it was we were, we wouldn't get headaches. I was prone to them. Especially, when I had to use so much power on such insignificant bugs.

I missed the old days when people did business in person and not through electronic boxes. Then you could bypass all the trouble of deciphering the tone of their voice and see in their eyes whether they were crooked or genuine.

Things were much simpler then.

Without knocking, my office door opened, and Piper sauntered into my office. "Don't mind me, just getting the trash."

I leaned up off my elbows to watch her move across my office like she owned the place instead of just being the maid of it. Her long blonde hair was up in a messy bun, giving me an unobstructed view of her long neck, and the hunger to taste her came raging forward. It didn't help that she wore a pair of cut-off shorts that practically showed off her backside and a bright pink tank top that read 'Bite me' with a cartoon set of fangs surrounding it. She didn't even seem bothered by my eyes on her as she bent over in front of me to gather my garbage. I shifted in my chair to hide my growing arousal.

"Miss Billings." I laced my fingers in front of me on the desk.

Piper looked up from the trash and hummed in my direction. Those pretty brown eyes were wide and surrounded by long eyelashes. She made the predator in me want to come out.

"What is this horrendous outfit you are wearing?"

Her brows furrowed for a moment, the trash bag in her hand poised to be taken out. Then her eyes dipped down to her chest, and her eyes widened in horror. Her delectable lips formed an o-shape as she turned toward me.

"Oh, my God. I totally forgot I was wearing this."

"Clearly," I mused and pushed back the urge to smile at her discomfort. "Do we need to have another discussion about the declaration for someone to 'bite you,' or is this your way of telling us you would like to be on tonight's menu?"

Piper's face flushed red, and she shook her head violently. "No, no. I didn't mean that. It's a joke, I swear." She gestured a hand on a tank top with an annoyed pinch of her brows. "I got it for Halloween one year after my friends kept pestering me to dress up with them."

She glanced up and locked eyes with me. With a huff, she stomped her foot like a petulant child before crossing her arms over her chest. It did nothing to cover up the words on her shirt and everything draw my attention to her breasts.

"I blame you and your workaholic ways. It's freaking noon. Shouldn't you be dead to the world already?" She waved a hand at me with a fiery glare.

"Yes, normally, I would be dead to the world, as you put it." I paused and let the words sink it. I watched with delight as her uncertainty whirled through her mind and across her face. She was so easy to read. It was almost like watching one of those television sets. Amusing, indeed. "However, while I might be a vampire, the rest of the world is not, and they sometimes require me to be available in the middle of the day."

She was quiet for a moment and then let out a little, "Oh." Shifting in place, she dropped her arms and gripped the trash bag tighter. "Well, then good for you. I'm going to go... clean something. That's right. Uh, bye."

I watched her hips sway in those tiny shorts as she marched to the office door she hadn't bothered to close. Before I could stop myself, I called out to her, "Miss Billings?"

"Uh, yeah?" She paused at the door without bothering to turn around and face me.

"Do not wear those shorts around my brothers," I warned her. "They do not have the restraint I do when seeing your lovely legs in such a provocative fashion."

She sniffed and put her nose in the air. "Well, it's not my fault they have no self-control. It doesn't give you the right to blame me because of my clothing choices."

Since her back was to me, I let a small smile grace my lips. "It is not the clothing choice, but the fact is that the less clothing you wear, the more we can scent your blood, and the artery in your inner thigh is most fragrant of them all."

I could see the blush rising up the back of her neck at my words, and it almost had me out of my seat and going to her. However, I curled my fingers into my hands, letting the pain my nails caused cool my need.

Instead of rushing off, she straightened her back and flipped me off. "That's not my problem either." Piper then stomped out of the office and slammed the door behind her.

I chuckled to myself as I listened to her grumble in the hallway. She had lost most of her timidness around me ever since the talk we had a few weeks ago. The topic had been about the matter of her self-pleasuring herself so loudly the whole house could hear her. I believe I had told her she sounded like a dying cow. That, of course, was untrue, but I had to do something to dissuade her, to ease the ache I felt every time I was around her. She had not taken my description well.

Now, Piper walked away from me when I wanted nothing more than to bend her over my desk and have my way with her. However, that would make me no better than my brothers who couldn't keep their cocks in their pants for longer than a week let alone a century. At least, I had Darren to stem off some of the constant need. Not that it was one-sided in the least. I enjoyed our time together as much as he did, but after a while, a little bit of female company would be nice.

Thankfully, my thoughts on our sexy little maid were cut short by the ringing of my phone. I picked it up and saw the caller flash across the screen. Valentine? Why would that bastard be calling at this time of day? Why was he calling period?

I never liked the man in the first place, but ever since he tried to take advantage of Piper, I'd grown to dislike him even more. If we didn't share a sire, one that currently favored Valentine, then I would have ignored the call altogether. But seeing as a snub to him would be a snub to our sire, I couldn't very well do so.

Pushing back my irritation, I pushed the answer button. "Hello, Valentine. What causes you to call me as such a late hour?"

Valentine's laugh poured through the phone, and I held back a shudder. "Don't pretend like you weren't already awake. We all know you can't stop working for a heartbeat."

"Yes, well, some of us cannot rely upon our sire to take care of us," I drawled out and leaned back in my chair. I pulled my long blonde hair over my shoulder and began to braid it while holding the phone against my face.

"You could as well if you came home." Valentine was constantly trying to persuade me to dissolve my house and rejoin the family, something I wouldn't do in a million years, even if they begged me. I'd spent my time under our sire's thumb long enough, and I wasn't about to go back there to subject my brothers to it again.

"I am perfectly content where I am but thank you for the offer. Now, if you could tell me the nature of your call, I would very much like to retire to my bed." I tried my best to be polite and not sound like I wanted to stab him in the back with a blunt stake while my fingers moved through my hair, looping one lock over the other.

Valentine chuckled. "Well, aren't we cranky? That little maid of yours ruffling your feathers again? How is she by the way? Still as lovely as ever?" The way he said it made me think he was licking his lips in anticipation of tasting her.

Not in this lifetime.

"She's fine," I let out in a clipped tone in the hoped of bringing him to his point sooner rather than later.

"Oh, I bet she is." Valentine let out a little dreamy sigh and then continued, "In any case, she is partly the reason I am calling. *He* wants to see you and your little maid."

I sat up straighter and dropped my partially finished braid so I could hold the phone more firmly. "When?"

"Next Sunday. Say eightish?"

I gritted my teeth and bit out, "That's quite short notice. I will have to pay extra to get the plane ready in time to—"

"Great," he practically crooned. "I'll see you then."

There was nothing but silence after that. I glared at the phone, not quite believing he had just hung up on me, but of course, he had. He was our sire's little errand boy. He delighted in causing pain and misery, especially if it benefited him.

Once upon a time, I was the favorite son. I was my sire's greatest achievement, and he wanted nothing more than to show me off to the world and take advantage of my gifts. Then one day, I saw what he was doing to me, to my brothers, and wanted no more of it. I requested our freedom... because nobody demanded anything from *him*... and, for some reason, he allowed it.

Ever since then, Valentine had taken my place up as the favorite son. It was something he relished in, and he took great pleasure in rubbing my face in it.

Not that I cared. I didn't want the position. He could have it and all the horrors that came with it.

With a sigh, I stood from my desk and adjusted my suit jacket before flipping off my desk light and walking to the door. After meticulously turning off the lights and closing up my room, I angled my head to the side to listen to where Piper had run off to.

I heard faint, off-key singing down the hallway in what sounded like Rayne's bedroom. Satisfied that she was truly occupied, I made my way down the stairs and then into the basement. There, I found all but two of my brothers asleep.

Marcus and Wynn sat at the couch playing a game of cards. When they heard me coming, they paused their game to glance my way.

"I was wondering when you would be coming to bed." Wynn laid his head against the back of the couch. "Did you have fun messing with Piper? I could hear her grumbling from down here."

I didn't bother to respond to his question. Wynn was nothing more than an immature child on the best of days, but if you threw in something he wanted, he upgraded to a jealous teenager. Not much of an improvement, but at least then you could talk some sense into him.

"If you would spend less time spying on Miss Billings and more time listening to my conversations, then you would know we have bigger problems to worry about." My words caused the two of them to focus on me more fully. "Valentine called."

"Again?" Wynn scoffed. "Tell him to fuck off. We aren't giving him Piper."

I removed my suit jacket and set it over the back of my desk chair near my bed. "This isn't about Piper, at least not entirely."

I thought about what he said as I sat down and removed my shoes. There was no doubt in my mind that the reason our sire wanted to see us after so long was because of Valentine running his mouth about our new employee. Our sire might not be a lover of women, but he never gave up the chance to take something that we wanted for himself, even if it was just to destroy it.

"Come on now, Antoine." Wynn huffed and leaned over the couch. "Don't leave us in suspense. What did the twat want?"

Letting out a long sigh, I turned to him and said, "We've been summoned."

"When?" Marcus asked.

I unbuttoned my shirt as I answered, "Sunday at eight."

Wynn whistled. "He didn't give us much time to get ready, huh?"

"No," I mused, "but then again. When *he* says jump, we say—"

"How high? I know. Just wish some vampire hunter would put a stake through that asshole's chest already and save us all the trouble." Wynn let out a dramatic sigh and collapsed on the couch. "We better prepare to leave then. Let our adorable maid know not to miss us too much while we're gone."

"No need for that." I grimaced. "She's coming with us."

"What?" Wynn sat up straighter as his brows shot to his forehead.

Nodding grimly, I moved over to my bed and laid down. I laced my fingers over my stomach and stared up at the ceiling. I could still hear Piper moving around the house and humming some tune from the radio. "Another one of Valentine's ideas, I'm sure of it."

"We'll have to be careful," Marcus added.

Closing my eyes, I murmured, "Yes, indeed."

CHAPTER 5
Piper

THE MASTERS WERE BEING suspicious today. Not that they weren't every day. I mean, they were vampires. Being mysterious was kind of their MO, but today they were even more paranoid than usual.

My day had started off like any other day. Up by seven. Took a shower where I did NOT give in to the urge to touch myself. Antoine had pretty much killed that desire with his comments about me sounding like a dying cow. One would think that I would moan even louder to spite him, but I was too mortified by the fact that they could hear me do it, anyway. If I did do it, I made sure it was midday, and I was as silent as the grave. No utterances of who I was thinking about or otherwise... which also brought on another dilemma.

Rayne.

A woman couldn't even masturbate in peace without worrying about someone catching snippets of what they're thinking about. I mean, it was bad enough they could hear me and smell me, but Rayne could literally see what I was fantasizing about. It really cooled one's desire, to say the least.

So, my showers were decidedly fast and cool, lest I have the urge take me. I then went downstairs and had breakfast with Darren. Once again, he asked me if I was going to tell the masters about my stalker.

It's not that I didn't want to tell them. It was more that I didn't want to worry them or give them a reason to fire me. I mean, they acted like they cared about me, but I didn't know how far that extended when coming up against one of their own.

I just didn't want to chance it. Better to ignore it and hope Valentine got bored.

So, after dodging Darren's questions, I went about my day cleaning as usual. Okay, so maybe I messed around and snooped through some of the other's rooms... like Antoine's. That guy was just too put together not to have some kind of embarrassing kink. Alas, I found nothing but business suits and perfectly lined-up loafers in his closet. A girl could die of boredom with how un-vampire-like these guys were. Really, the only saving grace was the occasional dinner party where they were certainly not eating steak and potatoes.

Tonight was one of those nights... or it was supposed to be. However, when I came down for dinner, Darren didn't try to rush me through my meal or hurry me back upstairs. Instead, he was sitting at the kitchen table with a cup of hot tea, something he only drank when he was upset, and the skin between his brows pinched together.

"What's going on?" I slid into the chair opposite of him a frown on my lips. "No dinner party tonight?"

Darren glanced up from his teacup only for a moment to acknowledge my presence before looking back to it. "No. It's been canceled."

I glanced at the kitchen where nothing had been prepared for us by Gretchen or any semblance of something I could grab to eat.

The oddities just kept coming.

"So..." I drew out. "Where is everyone? Big night out?"

With a shake of his head, Darren sighed and pulled his white gloves off to set them on the table. My eyes widened. I'd never seen Darren without his gloves, not even to wash the dishes. How he kept them from getting wet or ruined was beyond me. It was like watching someone taking off their pants, An oddly personal thing that I felt like I should avert my eyes for.

"The masters have taken their meals to the basement. They will be there all night and have asked not to be disturbed." He shot me a warning look before returning to his tea.

I inclined my head and sat there waiting for him to elaborate. Seeing that I wasn't getting anything else from him, I stood up and made my way to the fridge. Pulling it open, I searched through Gretchen's pre-made meals. Spaghetti. Meatloaf. Ah, chicken salad. That was quick and easy.

After grabbing the container, I snatched the bread on my way to the island. I placed my treasures on the top of the counter and went to retrieve a plate. While I was moving around and preparing my food, I could feel Darren's eyes on me. I wasn't sure why he was watching me. I wasn't doing anything out of the ordinary. It really started to bug me when I started to eat my sandwich and he was still staring.

"What?" I asked through a mouthful of sandwich. My question made Darren grimace, and I swallowed my food. "I mean, why are you looking at me like that?"

Darren stood and brought his teacup over to the sink, his hands still gloveless. "I'm waiting for the other shoe to drop."

"Huh?"

With a shake of his head, Darren washed his cup and put it in the drainer. "You are usually incessant in your questioning. You are the nosiest human I'd ever met, and yet you have yet to ask why they are spending the evening in the basement or anything else. You'll forgive me if prior experience has made me cautious."

I shrugged. "What can I say? I'm just not that interested in what they're doing down there." I took another large bite of my sandwich and chewed it around all the while Darren continued to stare at me. Swallowing my bite this time before I spoke, I sighed dramatically. "What now?"

Darren arched a brow. "So, you don't care at all what they are talking about down there?"

"No, I don't." I nodded firmly, proud of myself for being a mature adult.

"Even if they're talking about you?"

"What?!" I exclaimed. I dropped my sandwich on my plate and ran for the basement door. I wiggled the door handle and cursed. Locked. Not to be deterred, I pressed my face up against the door. The wood made my face cold, but I powered through it, urging my ears to be better. I listened for a few moments and tried to hear something anything.

What could they be talking about down there? What did I have to do with it? Did they find out about the vase in the guest bedroom? I hadn't meant to break it. I mean, who puts a decorative vase in a guest room? Especially one with breakable parts. That mermaid didn't need her tail, anyway.

Or maybe it was about Rayne and me? Did the little brat tell them about our kiss? Or even about the almost kiss in Allister's bathroom the other day? Oh, that sneaky little jerk wad. Can't kiss and keep his mouth shut. See if I ever kiss him again.

Oh! Maybe it's about the flowers? Darren told them about Valentine's flowers, and they are deciding on what to do about it. Would they confront Valentine? Or would they decide that I finally had caused one too many problems for them and fire me?

Oh, God. The not knowing was killing me!

"You're not going to hear anything through that door." Darren stood behind me, his hands behind his back. "That wood is so thick that you wouldn't hear a bomb go off down there."

"That just makes me wonder why they have a soundproof room," I argued with my hands on my hips. "What poor defenseless victim is down there begging for help but can't be heard through this thick ass door?"

Darren sighed, and his eyes closed for a second before opening them again. "One, the soundproofing is for them, not us. They can hear everything we do up here otherwise, and even with it, the door doesn't block every sound."

I suddenly thought of Antoine hearing me in my bedroom and flushed. "So, they should just build a metal container and be done with it."

Shaking his head, Darren pulled his gloves back on one finger at a time. "Metal containers are not easy to come by and harder still to install in a house as old as this one. We made do with what we have. Now, if you would come back to the kitchen, we can discuss this without disturbing the masters."

My eyes shot to the door and then back to Darren. I didn't want to leave in case he was wrong, that I would hear something eventually. Maybe they could hear me now and were being quiet until I left? I could be quiet, as quiet as a mouse. Perhaps then they would say something I could catch.

Ugh. I hated not knowing what was going on. I should be privy to what was discussed about my future!

"Please stop already. Just watching you fret is giving me a headache." Darren rubbed his temple with one hand, his eyes closing briefly. "If you come back to the kitchen, I think we still had some of that ice cream you enjoyed so much last time."

My ears perked up at the mention of ice cream. I was a sucker for sweets, and Darren knew it. "Fine play dirty, but I'll find out. I always do." I sniffed and marched passed him my head held high.

"I'm sure you will." Darren followed me with an exasperated tone. "Not even the mice's secrets are safe in this house."

"Pfft. Mice don't have secrets," I told him with a grin. "They whine over cheese."

CHAPTER 6
Rayne

MY BROTHERS AND I sat around the basement as we waited for Antoine to tell us what had happened. He sat as his desk he kept down stairs as usual not even bothered that we were waiting for him.

Antoine was a hard guy to read most days but he had been unusually guarded today. Even his mind was blocked from me, giving me no inkling of what he might be thinking.

Fortunately, while I had been sleeping my brothers hadn't. Marcus and Wynn already knew what news Antoine had gathered to tell us and they weren't being shy about hiding their thoughts.

We'd been summoned.

It wasn't a surprising announcement. Our sire could summon us at any moment, and we would have to rush to where ever he asked or face his wrath. No one wanted to enrage that old Russian bastard, least of all me.

I shuddered at the thought.

"Cold, brother?" Drake grinned cheekily at me from the back of the couch where he was perched next to his twin.

I flipped him off as I rolled my eyes, choosing to focus on Antoine instead. I couldn't get all the details from Wynn and Marcus, not unless they were actively thinking about those things.

Marcus was trying to match his face with his thoughts. Blank. Empty. A black void.

Wynn, however, grumbled more about having to put up with Theresa than having to see our sire. That was a sentiment I understood very well. That woman knew no shame and spread her legs for every and any vamp that would take her... sometimes even when they didn't want to. Wynn was the idiot for thinking he needed to prove he was truly irresistible and claim every woman in our sire's house, an act that caught Theresa's absolute attention. As sympathetic as I was, the situation was his own fucking fault.

"I'm sure you are all wondering why I have called you here after canceling tonight's festivities," Antoine droned on. He unbuttoned his jacket and slipped his hands into his pockets, but even then, he didn't lower himself to so much as lean on his desk. "As I told Marcus and Wynn earlier today, our sire has deemed it necessary for us come home for a visit."

"You mean that he summoned us." Drake and Allister said together and then snorted, crossing their arms over their massive chests at the same time, mirror images of themselves. It was scary sometimes how alike they were on the outside but how different they were on the inside.

Drake, for example, did not think in complete sentences and tended to curse far more in his mind than out loud. He thought about his biceps... a lot.

And Allister... Well, Allister was far more complex than he would lead others to believe. His mind wasn't full of frivolous things like his brother's. More often than not, Allister was thinking about the latest book he had read or something he heard on the news. It was refreshing to listen to his thoughts after all these years with Wynn and Drake. They thought way too much about themselves and women, always women. I thought I was the young one of the family, but apparently, you didn't get over the need for sex with age or maturity, something neither of them seemed to have in abundance.

"Yes," Antoine continued as he gave the twins a warning look. "We have been summoned. We are expected next Sunday at eight."

"Fuuuuuck." Allister drew out and shook his head. "You think he gave us enough notice?"

"Right?" Wynn nodded in agreement. "I hardly have time to cancel my plans."

Drake let out a rude sound. "Plans? You mean beating off to the thought of a little blonde maid? You can do that anywhere."

"Watch it, you," Wynn frowned, his jaw tightening, "or I'll make you fuck a lamp post... again."

Drake flinched and backed down at that.

Wynn grinned smugly. "Don't forget to tell them the best part, brother."

"The best part?" Drake and Allister straightened up as they looked back to Antoine.

I can't wait to see how they react to hearing our lord and master wants to meet Piper, Wynn thought. *They're going to—*

"What the fuck?" I shot up from my place on my bed. "What do you mean he wants to meet Piper? No." I sliced my arm through the air and glared. "No way. This is just some ploy for Valentine to try to mess with her again. You know it is!" As I went on my tirade, I stomped over to Antoine and stared him down.

Antoine let out an impatient sigh. "Do you think we haven't thought of that? We are well aware of what the leading cause of this summons may have been. However, if we didn't want Valentine to be so interested in our human, some of us should have been a bit let territorial last time he was here." His eyes narrowed on me.

I stood my ground and took a step forward. "You surely aren't blaming me for this? If I hadn't stepped in when I had, Valentine would have bitten Piper."

"Maybe you should have let him," Marcus murmured.

I spun around and gaped at Marcus. "You can't mean that?"

"I'm with Rayne." Wynn lazily gestured to me from the bed. "Even I wouldn't dare give anyone to Valentine, even to let him just bite them." Wynn shuddered. "Ugh, he doesn't even let them feel pleasure in the bite. He enjoys hurting them."

"Exactly." I whipped back around to Antoine. "Would you in your right mind ever give someone under your protection to that monster? She's our maid. You convinced her to stay when she wanted to leave. How could you think for even a second that we could do that to her?"

Antoine watched me for a moment without saying a word before breaking his gaze away to scan the others in the room. "Do you all feel this way as well?"

Wynn stood to his feet. "Indubitably."

Drake and Allister inclined their heads, and Drake added, "Even if I weren't fond of the little minx, I wouldn't give anything to Valentine just out of spite."

"I second that." Allister smacked his brother on the shoulder. "That slimy ass can suck my hairy balls before I ever let him touch a hair on our girl's head."

The twins chuckled between them... but my eyes were on Marcus, the one who had suggested we should hand her over in the first place, the one who didn't really seem to care if Piper stayed or went, lived or died. If our decision wasn't unanimous, I wasn't sure what Antoine would do, but I would spirit Piper away if I had to. I wouldn't give her over to Valentine, even if it meant leaving my brothers and all I knew behind.

Marcus stared at us for a long moment and then, in perfectly Marcus fashion, jerked his head in consent.

Fucking dick.

"Are you sure?" Antoine cocked a brow at Marcus. "You were just talking about getting rid of her? Now you want to change your mind?"

Marcus shrugged a shoulder. "I am obviously outvoted. I will not be the piece that pulls this family apart. If you wish the human woman to stay, then she stays."

"Very well." Antoine turned to the rest of the room. "Now that it has been settled, who would like to be the one to tell her?"

Drake and Allister burst out laughing. They waved Antoine off, threw themselves over the side of the couch, and picked up their game controllers. Obviously, they weren't going to do it.

"We do have another issue," Wynn mentioned. The twins didn't even bother looking away from the game they had begun to play.

"Besides figuring out how to keep Valentine and his nasty fangs off Piper?" I asked with a sneer. "Please, I'm all ears."

"Well, if you would rein in your attitude, I'll tell you," Wynn snarked as he glared at me. I huffed and then gestured for him to continue. "To keep Piper safe from Valentine and our mercurial sire, I suggest we do a little more than a claiming this time."

"What do you suggest?" Antoine arched a brow, clearly interested in what Wynn was talking about.

A sudden image was shoved into my mind before I was ready for it, one of Wynn and Piper lying on a bed. They were nude, of course, and he had his mouth wrapped around her neck as he plunged into her with both fangs and dick.

"Geez, fuck, Wynn." I shook my head as I slapped the side of it. "Warn a guy before you start fucking someone in your mind. Shit."

Wynn gave me a sheepish grin and lifted a shoulder. "Sorry, mate. My desire got away from me."

"I'll bet that's all that got away," I grumbled and shook my head once more. "So, besides screwing her, what exactly do you plan on doing to protect her?"

"He wants to bind her." Antoine stepped up beside me. "Like I have done Darren, correct?"

As Wynn sat up on the bed, he pushed his dark hair over his shoulder. "Yes. It's the obvious choice, isn't it? Bind her to one of us and then Valentine is a moot point."

"He has a point," Drake called over his shoulder without taking his eyes off the game. He was clearly bearing his twin.

"It would keep unwanted attention off of her and satisfy our sire," Antoine mused as he rubbed his chin between his fingers, his brows furrowing together in thought.

"But do you really want to listen to her bitch at you for all eternity?" Allister added after finally pausing the game, much to Drake's dismay. "She's hot, don't get me wrong, I'd love to get a piece of that action."

I gritted my teeth against his words but didn't call him out on it.

"Yeah, what he said." Drake pointed at his brother, game controller in hand. "It's obvious she's attracted to us. I mean, who wouldn't be, right?" He chuckled and bumped fists with his twin. "But adding a woman to the family isn't the same as adding someone like Darren."

"True." Wynn nodded and then glanced at Marcus. "What about you? You must have an opinion past saving ourselves the headache."

Marcus's nostrils flared before he bit out, "Bind her and bring her to heel."

I barked a laugh that kept going until all my brothers had turned to look at me. Bent over at the waist, slapping my thigh, I wiped the tears forming at my eyes.

"Oh, God. Sorry. Hold on a second. Wow. Uh." I took a second to catch my breath and then dragged a hand through my shaggy hair. "If you think binding Piper to one of us will bring her to heel, you are asking for an eternity of misery because that's just not going to happen."

"Ah, yes. She is quite the spitfire." Drake stared off into space as his head filled with the image of Piper screaming at him for something or another. Socks, I think.

She's going to be a hellion in bed, was Wynn's sole thought.

"Really?" I rolled my eyes over to Wynn with a flat tone. "That's all you can think about right now? We're deciding Piper's future... the rest of her life which could very well be an eternity in this very basement, and you're thinking about how her personality will transfer into bed?"

Wynn smirked. "What can I say? You have your priorities, I have mine."

While my fist itched to punch a hole through Wynn's face, Antoine stepped between us and blocked my view of his smug face. "You bring up a good point, Rayne. We should not be making these decisions for her. Miss Billings... Piper... needs to decide for herself what she would like to do. Whether she would like to continue working here for us or if she would rather continue on with her life."

"Leaving here will not protect her from Valentine," I countered with a frown. "Even if we give her up, Valentine will take that as his chance to hunt her down and take her, just to spite us."

"Regardless," Antoine retorted, "it is not our decision to make. We cannot take away someone else's free will to make things easier on ourselves."

The mention of free will made us all grow silent. Free will was something all of us valued deeply. It was one of the reasons we had voted to leave our sire's home. There, the very notion of saying no was ridiculous. You did what the sire wanted regardless of your own personal feelings. Meaning that if you preferred women but he wanted to fuck you... well, you said, 'How do you want me?' If he wanted you to blow his visiting friend from overseas with the exceptionally hairy balls, then you bought a whole lot of toothpaste and took a knee.

Free will above all else.

CHAPTER 7
Piper

MY FACE WAS STILL pressed up against the wood of the door to the basement when it suddenly opened. I jolted back but not fast enough, and the corner of the door whacked into my foot.

"Shit!" My eyes watered and my hand grabbed my foot as I jumped in place to staunch the pain.

"Piper, my Lord! I apologize. I didn't know you were there." Wynn reached out to me, holding me by the shoulders so that I didn't fall over. His blue eyes were soft with concern.

"It's fine." I gave him a pained smile and tried to wave him off. "It's my fault."

"No, no. It's completely mine. I should have—"

"What? Used your x-ray vision to see that I was pressing my ear up against the door like a nosy busy body?" I scoffed and laughed.

Wynn offered me a small smile. "Well, I suppose that would have been asking a bit much. I already have so many alluring qualities." He lifted his hand up with a smirk. "Immortality. Speed. A face women cry for."

"Cry out in disgust, you mean." Drake chuckled and clapped his hand on Wynn's shoulder, the twin a head taller than the flirtatious vampire before me.

Wynn feigned hurt as he placed his hand on his chest. "I beg your pardon. I would have you know I have never made a woman... or man, for that matter... want anything other than to cry out in pleasure and delight." His eyes turned to me with a pleading sort of look. "You must believe me, Piper."

I covered my mouth with the back of my hand, my hurt foot all but forgotten. "If you say so."

"Ugh!" Wynn clasped both hands at his chest. "And the final stab to the heart. You pain me so, my dear Piper. I would not think you would have pity on a poor humble vampire."

Drake and I met each other's eyes over Wynn and broke out into fits of laughter. While Wynn complained about how heartless we were, footsteps bounded up the stairs from the still-open basement door. When Rayne appeared at the top of the stairs with Allister close behind him, my laughter was cut off as I fell into a coughing fit.

"Piper?" Wynn placed a hand on my back. "Are you alright? Do you need a drink of water?"

I waved him off with one hand and covered my mouth with the other one. "No. N—" I coughed. "I'm okay," I gasped and winced as my voice cracked.

"If you're sure, but let's get you some, just in case." Wynn began to usher me toward the kitchen without giving me a chance to say no. The others followed behind us, seemingly more interested in what was going on with us than doing whatever it was they had planned to do.

Wynn sat me down at the kitchen island and moved to the sink. I kept my eyes away from Rayne as he leaned against the fridge and watched me with a focus that made me squirm.

"What was so funny before?" Rayne asked.

I glanced toward Rayne for a second, taking in the tight t-shirt he was wearing and low riding sweat pants before my mind drifted off to the bathroom where we'd almost kissed. What would have happened had I let him kiss me again? Would it have been like last time, aggressive and overpowering like he wanted to swallow me whole and make sure everyone damn well knew I belonged to him? My body hummed with the thought of it, not particularly displeased by the notion.

Rayne sucked in a sharp breath.

The realization of what I had just been thinking caught up to me, and my eyes briefly locked with his before I jerked them away, my face burning. I had to be more careful with my thoughts around him... around all of them, for that matter. They might not all be able to read my mind, but they sure could read my scent, and I knew, to my utter mortification, it was screaming that Piper was thinking dirty, dirty thoughts.

Luckily, Wynn placed the cup of water in front of me, and I had a reason not to speak. I picked up the cup, taking small sips as I avoided the questioning gaze of the assembled brothers. Thick tension filled the kitchen for a few moments before Drake cleared his throat to cut through it.

"So, eavesdropping, were you?" He leaned his large bicep on the edge of the island next to me, a shit-eating grin on his face. Drake had me blocked on one side while Allister slid into the chair next to me, effectively putting me in a hot twin sandwich.

Rayne snorted.

My eyes shot to him and narrowed. "Stay out of my head."

He lifted a shoulder and offered me an unapologetic smile. "I can't help it. You think too loud."

"Don't feel bad." Allister leaned toward me his elbow on the counter. "He does it to all of us. You just have to learn to block him out."

"How?" I glanced between them.

"Try to clear your mind, think of nothing. You are nothing. So, he sees nothing," Drake pantomimed a fortune teller with his hands around an invisible crystal ball, his voice low and dramatic.

I giggled and covered my mouth with my hand.

Drake dropped his hands with a smirk and a waggle of his brows. "And if that doesn't work, just think of something utterly repulsive, and he usually gets the hint." The twins shot a look in unison at Rayne where he had been watching us with narrowed eyes.

The edges of my lips curled up, and I brought the image of wanting to lick the toilet seat before I'd want to kiss him again. Rayne's eyes widened for a second before narrowing into slits. Without a word, he pushed up off the fridge, shook his head, and stomped out of the room.

"See?" Drake clapped me on the back. "Easy."

"I'm curious though," Wynn mused and angled over the edge of the island across from me. "What did you think about that angered him so?'

I picked up my water and took another sip before shrugging a shoulder. "Just something utterly disgusting." I winked at them but didn't divulge further.

They glanced between themselves and then chuckled, the sound sinking into my skin and making me shudder. God, save me from hot vampire men.

"So, what was your meeting about?" I asked, not bothering with pleasantries anymore. I laced my fingers in front of me and pretended to be a purely innocent bystander who would never think to eavesdrop on them.

82

Wynn gave a noncommittal wave of his hand. "Oh, this and that. You know, vampire things."

My brows rose. "Vampire things?" My nose crinkled. "Like blood and who's turn it was to shave the other's face?"

Drake and Allister busted out laughing and almost fell out of their seats. Once Drake managed to catch his breath, he swiped his finger beneath his eye. "Oh, I think I like you, Piper Billings. You're far more entertaining than any of our previous help, especially Darren."

"Oh, I don't know." I grinned broadly. "You might want to watch what you say, Darren can wield a vegetable knife like a pro. I'd be afraid about getting on his bad side."

This only made them laugh harder. Even Wynn joined in this time. The sound of his laughter made my lower parts clench deliciously. I took a long drink of my water, half tempted to dump it on top of my head to cool my libido for a moment.

"What's so funny?" I asked as my lips tipped down in a frown.

"My apologies, Piper," Wynn told me with that cultured accent of his. "We are not laughing at you. It is just the thought of Darren being a threat to any of us is amusing."

"Why?"

"Because he's bound to us," Wynn explained.

"No. He's bound to Antoine. There's a difference," Allister pointed out with a stern look before turning a small smile my way. "I'm Allister, by the way. I know we have technically met but I wasn't exactly being myself."

I glanced down at his hand for a moment, my brows scrunched together in confusion. "You used to be the quiet guy who didn't know how to put a sentence together in front of me, and here you are, cracking jokes. What gives?" I cocked a brow at him as I slid my hand into his larger one.

"We were trying not to use our abilities on you to make you like us," Allister explained as he shrugged a shoulder. "Mine is harder to not use than the others."

I shot a look at the rest of them. "So... what are your abilities then? I found out that Rayne could read minds from Darren."

Drake laughed. "Boy doesn't know when to leave well enough alone."

"Right." I nodded curtly, then looked to Wynn. "I think I know what yours is, but I'm not sure what to call it." I flushed as I remembered his hands on me and the overwhelming need to have him touching me, kissing me. I was a healthy woman with a regularly sized appetite for sex, but around him, it just didn't seem to have a limit.

Wynn gave me a lazy, self-satisfied grin. "I am so honored that you would think of me so often." He reached a hand across the table and took mine in his own, stroking it in what most would call an innocent way, but they wouldn't see the hot, needy desire that came rampaging through me just from those small strokes. It was like he was touching me in places I couldn't reach myself.

I sucked in a breath and closed my eyes before jerking my hand from his grasp. I dipped my head, my face heated again as I waved him off. "Stop it."

"My apologies." I could hear the smile in his voice, and it did nothing to lessen the need inside of me. My clit pulsated against my jeans, and I shifted in my seat in a vain attempt to quench the need for friction.

Clearing my throat, I opened my eyes to look at Drake. "So, uh, what about you? Your powers, I mean! It was that thing you tried to do to me that first day, isn't it?"

Allister banged on the island, and I jumped in place as he pointed an accusatory finger at his twin. "I knew you cheated!"

Drake merely gave his brother a cheeky grin. "What can I say? I can't help myself.

Besides," his eyes dropped from his brothers to meet mine, "if you had been faced with such a lovely woman in such a vulnerable position as I had, you might have done the same."

I swear my face was going to be permanently red from all the blushing these guys caused me. The first time I had run into Drake while cleaning, he had come out of the bathroom only clad in a tiny white towel. It did nothing to hide that glorious body he was hiding beneath his clothes, and Drake had known it. He teased me and flirted merciless with me, and when that didn't work, he used some kind of charm against me. The next thing I knew, I was a bumbling fool, unable to say no or even recognize what the hell was going on. Thankfully, Marcus had shown up and stopped anything from happening.

Still, it was embarrassing as all get out.

"So that's your power? Being able to charm the panties off anyone?" I cocked my head to the side. "Seems kind of... unneeded?"

Drake frowned his brows furrowed. "What do you mean?"

I sighed and gestured at him. "Come on now. You own a mirror, right? You're sexy as hell. There's no way you need magic to get any girl to drop their panties for you."

A cocky smirk found its way onto his face, and I half-wished to take my words back. Me and my big mouth.

"You think I'm sexy, huh?" A dimple flashed in his cheek as he waggled his brows in an exaggerated way.

I threw my hands up in defeat. "If you're sexy, then your brother is too." I pointed my thumb back at Allister.

Drake shrugged and pursed his pouty lips. "That's okay. I don't mind sharing."

My eyes widened, and my mouth formed a large o-shape. "Do you guys do that?" I slowly swiveled back and forth in my seat. "You know... share? A lot."

Allister's blue-green eyes met mine, and a slow smile moved up his lips. "When the mood strikes... but it's not just us."

I didn't understand. My gaze moved to Wynn and then back to the twins. "You guys all share? Like, just blood or sex too?" I didn't know why I was torturing myself by asking any of this. It wasn't like they were going to do that with me or anything. Still, I had to know.

Wynn flashed a fang-toothed grin. "Not just me, lovely. We have been together for a very long time and have dabbled in all that there is."

"Wow." That's all I could say. I couldn't even comprehend the vast amount of experience these guys had. I mean, I wasn't a slut or anything, but I wasn't a nun either. I'd had my fair share of experience, but the way these guys were talking about it made me wonder how much I didn't know.

To give myself time to think, I picked up my glass and took another drink. When I sat it back down, I asked, "Even Antoine? And Marcus?"

Drake snorted. "Especially Marcus."

"That man is such a freak," Allister added in from behind me, "and let's not even get started on Rayne."

"Okay, that's enough, already." Rayne marched back into the kitchen and stopped at the edge of the island. "You're freaking her out on purpose now. Just tell her what she needs to know, so she has a real reason to worry."

I frowned at Rayne and then moved to the others. "What reason? Am I getting fired?" My hands started to sweat, and my heart raced at the prospective losing one of the best jobs I ever had. "I swear I haven't broken anything in like a week. Okay, that's a lie. I broke a plate yesterday, but it was hot. I didn't know the microwave would make the plate hot."

"Piper, calm down," Allister's voice murmured in my ear, and all at once my body did as he asked.

My heart slowed, and the anxiety disappeared in a snap. As I sagged in my chair, I slowly turned to Allister with a lopsided grin.

"So, that's your power. You're like a literal panty whisperer. I could see how you'd hide them." I found myself nodding, unable to stop.

With a laugh at my expense, Allister took my shoulders in his hands, then moved them to my face so as to stop my head from moving. "It's a dangerous power that can be used for good or evil."

"More like for perversion," Drake snapped from behind me. "Can't even think of getting the girl with this jerk around. One little whisper from him, and there go your chances. I have to actively put on my charm, but this guy doesn't even think about it, and it happens. Sometimes on accident!"

I was still a bit loopy from Allister's ability and had to shake my head to clear it. Once I felt a little more in control, my eyes widened, and I slipped out of my chair to back away from the four of them. "Um, sorry. I just... I need a minute."

Allister's eyes saddened, but he nodded.

After taking a few deep breaths, I looked to Wynn, the only one I deemed safe to talk to at the moment. "What do I need to know?"

Wynn let out a long sigh. "We've been summoned."

"Summoned?" I arched a brow. "Like you have jury duty or something?"

Rayne scoffed. "I wish."

"No," Wynn shook his head. "Not like jury duty. Our sire, the one who made us, has requested our presence."

"Requested?" Drake drawled out with a twist of his lips. "More like demanded. You don't say no to him."

"Okay, but what does that have to do with me?" I placed a hand on my chest and waited for the other shoe to drop. They wouldn't be suspiciously avoiding the subject if it wasn't something bad. I just hoped it wasn't the 'losing my job; kind of bad... or worse the 'Valentine was coming for another visit' kind of bad.

"Valentine won't be a problem," Rayne told me, and my eyes snapped to him. I started to tell him to stay out of my head again, but he held his hands up. "I know. I know. I'm sorry, but there's a lot to cover and not a whole lot of time." He pointed his thumb at the others. "And these assholes are taking too long."

"So, you tell me." I crossed my arms over my chest and cocked my hip to the side. "What's wrong with being summoned that has to do with me?'

"You're coming too," Rayne says matter-of-factly.

Now that wasn't something, I thought I was going to hear. Why in the world would I come with them to meet their sire? Didn't normal maids stay behind on trips like this? Well, this wasn't a normal household, to begin with, so maybe they didn't.

"Okay? So, I have to dress up like a Lolita again? Is that the bad news?" I couldn't believe how hopeful I sounded to have to put on that tight, degrading outfit again. How far I had fallen.

"Oh, you'll have to wear something but probably not that." Drake sniffed as he tried to repress a smile.

Wynn shot Drake a look before holding his hands open in front of him. "Our sire has specifically requested your presence, no doubt because Valentine has shown interest in you. He's probably gone back and told our sire that an unbound human is living with us."

"Okay, so now I have to meet the parents?" I asked, hoping that it was going to be a hi-bye kind of situation, and I would leave with my life and hopefully blood intact.

"Not exactly." Wynn shook his head. "If you are not bound to one of us, then our sire could decide that we have to give you to Valentine. Though Rayne told Valentine he had claimed you as his, you're still in a position to be taken."

"I don't understand." I scratched the side of my face. "You mean that being claimed is lower on your crazy totem pole than being bound? So, even though Rayne 'claimed me' that Valentine can still steal me away from you? What if I don't want to go with him?"

The vampires stared at me for a long moment before Wynn spoke up. He seemed to be the go-to spokesperson for the group when Antoine wasn't around. That was fine by me because Antoine was an ass and didn't make anything sound nicer than it was.

Wynn was also prettier.

Rayne smirked at that, so I gave him the stink eye to let him know I know he had been peaking in my head. I envisioned licking the toilet bowl again. When he flinched, I felt a smug bit of satisfaction and paid more attention to Wynn's words.

"You have a choice to make, Piper," Wynn told me with an apologetic air. "You can continue to work here for us, or you can find a new job. Of course, we will give you a good reference and even help you find one. If we can use our powers for one thing, it would be for this."

"Yeah!" Drake shoved a fist in the air. "We can totally find you a new place... though I'd hate to see you leave." His lower lip stuck out a bit as he blinked those long lashes at me.

I giggled and shook my head. "Why would I leave? I mean, being bound can't be that bad right? Darren seems to enjoy it." I paused for a second and thought about it. "Actually, I don't know if he enjoys it or not. He's kind of hard to read. Darren seems more like the type that would enjoy deep cleaning."

The men nodded in agreement before Wynn added, "Sadly, I have to say that is an astute assessment. That attitude is probably one of the reasons Antoine was so drawn to him in the first place. They both have a no-nonsense mentality, and they get along remarkably. However," he drew out and glanced at his brothers, "... being bound isn't just about keeping other vampires away from you. It's being with us. Forever."

"F-forever?" My brows shot up to my hairline, and my mouth dropped open.

"Yes." Allister nodded. "When you're bound, you'll be connected to the other person's life force. You won't die until they have. Meaning you could quite literally—"

"Live forever." I finished for him with a gulp. I now remembered Darren telling me something along those lines. Living forever? That wasn't something I'd ever thought about before. Certainly, nothing I ever wanted. My life up until this point had been pretty boring, a very take it or leave it existence that I only saw going downhill.

Until now. Moving into the mansion and working with these men, these vampires, had been the most excitement I'd had in my entire human life. Neither my family nor my friends, those little I had, made me want to get up in the morning and be a better person, a better version of me.

But here? I had a schedule. A purpose. A reason to get up and do my job to the best of its ability. Sure, my bosses were vampires and fed on humans, but that didn't mean they were bad guys. Besides, they weren't bad to look at either.

Rayne coughed, and my eyes shot to him.

Fuck. I'd done it again. Rayne had heard every single thing that had just gone through my mind. I hated it. I made every inch of me clench up, and the walls constrict around me. I needed privacy. I needed a break.

"I need to get out of here."

I shook my head and turned on my heel, barging up the back stairs before they could react. I kept going until I was safe behind my bedroom doors and even then, I knew I wasn't truly alone. They could hear me down there, moving around, maybe even breathing, but at least now, my thoughts were my own.

CHAPTER 8
Rayne

AS I WATCHED PIPER'S expression turn from contemplative into full-blown panic, I wanted to reach out and comfort her, to tell her that it wasn't as bad as she thought it would be. However, my reaction to her thoughts only reminded her that I had been listening... again.

I wanted to hate myself for it, but my power was part of who I was. I couldn't turn it off. And at this particular moment, Piper was thinking far too loudly for me to ignore her, not that I had wanted to.

Piper had been on my mind ever since she came to work for us. I just couldn't get her out of my head. At first, it had only been a perverse curiosity, as a new human toy to torment and runoff. When she didn't back down, not even when she found out we were vampires, that curiosity turned into something more.

Now, I couldn't stop thinking about her for a whole other reason. I wanted to see her. I wanted to be near her. To smell her scent. To touch her hair. Kiss her.

It had been a mistake to kiss her and taste her blood even if it was to save her from Valentine because now, I wanted more, not just her blood though I wanted that as well. I was a vampire for crying out loud. But I also wanted to feel her lips against mine, to hear her heart quicken as I pressed her to my chest. That soft body of hers had melded into mine so perfectly that I had woken up from a dead sleep dreaming of her. Yes, it'd given me more than one embarrassing awakening that had not gone unnoticed by my brothers.

"Dude, uncool." Drake shook his head and slipped off his chair. "At least fucking pretend not to listen. She's not used to this yet."

"I can't help it," I muttered as I leaned my forehead against the cool tile of the countertop. "Her thoughts are just so different."

"How so?" Wynn asked. His black hair was all I could see from my position.

"Faster for one," I huffed a laugh, "and chaotic. She jumps from one thought to the next like nothing I've ever seen."

"So, like how she talks?" Allister pointed out, and we couldn't help but laugh, a thankful reprieve from the tension.

I sat up and stared at my brothers, a serious tone coming over my voice. "She's freaking out. I don't know if she's going to want to do it."

"Of course, she's upset." Drake scoffed and waved a hand around at us. "None of us reacted positively the first time we found out we were going to live forever, and none of us had a choice. At least she has one and the time to think about what to do."

Allister inclined his head to agree with his twin. "Exactly. Give her time. We have a week. Then she can decide."

"But Antoine isn't going to want to wait that long. We need to prepare," I argued and dragged a hand through my messy hair, making it even worse. "If she's going to be bound, then we need to do it soon, so she has time to adjust."

"You mean for her to freak the fuck out even more." Drake snorted and rolled his eyes. "That's all well and good, but this isn't an easy decision. She's not dying. She could very well tell us all to fuck off and get another job."

We quieted at that thought. None of us wanted to see Piper go, especially not me... or Wynn. We were both already emotionally invested in her, and the twins were well on their way. They liked her for her spunk and her smart mouth. Plus, she was hot. I couldn't disagree with them for any reason they had for liking her.

At least they hadn't tasted her yet, not like I had. If they had, they'd already be head over heels for her.

Piper's blood was like nothing I'd ever tasted before. It wasn't good or bad, but it also didn't have that neutral flavor that some humans had when they straddled the moral line. No, she was like dark chocolate, sweet with a bitter after taste that you think you don't like but keep ending up coming back for.

And oh, did I want more.

"So, should we go talk to her?" Allister asked. "I could be persuasive in our favor."

"No way." I jumped in and slammed my hand down on the counter. "We're not forcing her to pick us. This is her choice. If we take that away from her..."

"She'll resent us for the rest of her long, long life." Wynn let out a remorseful breath. "We must let her choose and deal with the consequences as best we can."

While Wynn spoke as if he was leaving the decision up to her, he already had a plan in his mind to help her move her decision in the right direction, one that I could get wholeheartedly behind.

As I backed away from the island, I shoved my hands into my pockets and started for the kitchen door. "I'm going to go take a shower. Get some of the basement's stink off me."

My brothers waved me off as if they hadn't even heard me. They were all too caught up in their own thoughts to care about what I was doing. Perfect for me.

I headed up the stairs two at a time, listening for the sound of my other brothers. Marcus was still downstairs watching some nature show while Antoine, of course, was in his office... but with Darren.

My face reddened at the sounds they weren't trying to hide during their exploits. You'd think after all these years that I'd be used to it, but it still embarrassed me all the same. I blamed my parents. They were highly religious and thought that anything to do with sex was a sin. Even having it to make babies was borderline sinful in their eyes. If you're going to procreate, you better not enjoy it.

Fuck that.

I'd been so happy to become a vampire and get out from under their thumb. The first thing the twins had done was take me to a club where I spent the night drinking blood and discovering that sex was not something to be ashamed about but to be enjoyed to the fullest.

When I reached the top of the stairs, I paused and almost went to my bedroom to take the shower I had said I would... but at the last minute changed my mind and turned left toward Piper's bedroom.

I slowly approached her door and strained my ears to hear her inside. She wasn't crying. That was good at least, right?

What Piper was doing was pacing. I could hear the shuffle of her feet from one side of the room to the other. Her thoughts were even more chaotic than before, running through all kinds of crazy scenarios that would never happen even in our wildest dreams.

I thought that leaving her alone to think about the situation was a good idea, but the thoughts she was having were all wrong. She was thinking of all the bad and none of the good. I couldn't have that.

I knocked on her door three times and then waited.

Piper had stopped pacing at the first knock. Her mind still raced, but now, she was wondering who was at the door and if she could pretend not to be there.

"I can hear your heart beating," I said just loud enough to be heard through the door.

I almost laughed when she tried to slow her heartbeat down so I couldn't hear her. Then she realized how stupid that was because I still already knew she was in there. Finally, her mind went blank.

My brows furrowed as I tried to figure out what she was doing. I inched closer to the door and angled my head toward the surface. Before my face could touch it, the door swung open, and Piper's annoyed face stood inches from mine.

Leaning back, I tucked my hands into my jeans and flipped my head up to get my hair out of my face. "Hey, I just wanted to—"

"I'm fine, thanks. Bye." She tried to shut the door, but I shoved my foot in the way. After narrowing her eyes on that offending limb, she flicked her gaze up to me. "Move your foot."

"No."

"I have no issue hurting you. You'll heal in like five seconds flat, anyway." The dry tone of her voice told me how serious she was about it. That didn't bode well.

"I know, but I just needed to see you." I sighed and dragged my hand through my hair. Her eyes darted to the movement.

God, he has nice hair. I wonder if it's as soft as it looks.

I forced myself not to smile at her thoughts and shifted closer to her, trying to look contrite. "I wanted to apologize for earlier. I realize that I made assumptions based on a special circumstance and should have asked you how you felt about me kissing you before trying to do it again."

Her mouth dropped open slightly, then she clamped it shut with a curt nod. "Thanks. Is that it?"

She really wasn't going to make this easy, was she?

"That's it?" I gaped at her. "I apologize, and you don't have anything else to say? Nothing at all?"

Crossing her arms over her chest, Piper popped one hip out. "I don't know. Do I? You're the mind reader."

Fuck off, you pervy dick.

I didn't flinch at her thoughts, I didn't want her to know I was listening. Instead, I leaned forward until I was a hair's breadth away. "I don't need to read your thoughts to know you liked that kiss."

"Wh-what do you mean?" She blinked rapidly and wet her lips.

I smirked as I reached out a hand to push Piper's hair back from her face, my fingers tickling along her cheek. "You don't need to be a mind reader to see how you react to me. Even now, your heart rate is increasing. Your skin is warming to my hand on your face as you fight the urge to lean into my touch."

She let out a little gasp and tried to move away, but I wasn't done yet. I slipped my arm around her waist and brought us flush against each other. Piper's hand came up to my chest, but when she didn't immediately push me away, I let out a low rumble in my throat.

"I don't need to read your mind to hear your blood rushing to the junction between your thighs."

Her hooded eyelids flipped up to meet my heated gaze. "That's not fair." Her words came out low and husky. "You have the advantage."

I pushed my hips against hers to grind my erection into her. "You really think I could hide how you make me feel?"

Her throat bobbed as she swallowed, and her scent spiked with desire once more. "You did a good enough job before."

I let a small smile slid up my lips as I leaned my head down to her. "That was before this..." I pressed my mouth to hers to capture her lips with mine. She didn't kiss me back immediately but let out a small sigh like she'd been waiting all day for this moment. In a way, I suppose she was.

The hands on my chest crept up until they wrapped around my neck. She pressed herself more firmly against me and kissed me back for all she was worth. I let my hands drift up and down her back before settling on her butt. I groaned and tried to get even closer to her.

Fuck. Just kissing her was addicting. I couldn't tell if it was blood lust or regular lust that had me craving her, but one of them was responsible for what I did next.

As I grabbed one of her delectable thighs, I threw it over my hip and turned us so that her back was against the door. For a second, she let me hold her there, kissing me and rocking her hips in rhythm with mine. However, I was so caught up in her that I wasn't listening to her mind. So, when those hands that had been pulling me closer started to push me away, I let out a surprised grunt.

"What? What's wrong?" I tried to touch her face and get her to look at me, but she wouldn't.

"I can't. Just don't." She pushed me away and shook her head. Her blonde hair covered her face so I couldn't get a real read on her. "Please just go. I want to go to bed."

"But Piper..." I tried again, but she shut the door in my face. Huffing out a growl, I threw my hands up in the air and stomped down the hall. What the fuck had just happened?

CHAPTER 9
Piper

WHEN I WOKE UP the next morning, I knew the day was going to be a bad one. For one, my head ached. My stomach clenched like it was trying to eat me from the inside out which only meant one thing.

My period had arrived with a vengeance.

As I rolled out of bed, I groaned and palmed my forehead. This sucked. I hated having my period most months, but this month, it seemed to want to kill me.

I glared menacingly down at my uterus. "It's not my fault I'm not pregnant. Stop growling at me."

"Miss Billings?"

My head jerked up from my lower half to the closed bedroom door. "Darren?"

The butler let out an impatient sigh, and I could literally feel the condescension in his voice. "Who else would it be at this hour?"

At his words, my eyes moved to the clock by my bed. Eight-thirty! I bolted out of bed and hurried to my dresser. As I pulled out my clothes for the day, I spoke to Darren. "I'm so sorry. I didn't hear my alarm go off."

"Apparently," Darren drolled on. "Well, I have my own chores to do, so see to it you get to yours. We have more than enough to do before leaving for the summoning."

Without you slacking off. I knew what he was saying without actually speaking it. I'd screwed up, all because of my stupid period. However, if I thought about it, this was the first and only time I'd been late since I started the job. It was something I should be proud of, and I wouldn't be a child and shove in Darren's face, no matter how much he made me want to.

"I'll be down in a moment," I called out through the material of my shirt as I pulled it over my head. "Just give me five minutes."

My stomach tightened unexpectedly, and I winced. "I mean, ten. Give me ten."

"Very well."

Darren's footsteps moved down the hall, and I sighed. After grabbing a pair of stretchy lounge pants, I headed to the bathroom. Hey, if I had to work while blotted and cramping, I was going to do it comfortably.

As I went through my daily routine of brushing my hair into a ponytail and brushing my teeth, my mind drifted to last night. Rayne and that kiss. My fingers crept up to my lips, brushing against them in remembrance. It had been quite a kiss, not quite the same as the first one but still just as consuming.

While a part of me panicked at the idea of getting involved with a vampire who acted more like a teenager than the century-year-old man he was, another part of me wanted to do it again. Even in my miserably uncomfortable state, my body lit on fire with the thought of pressing up against that body again.

I shook my head and slapped myself on the face. "Knock it off, Piper. You have work to do… and Antoine would kill you. Probably literally."

I nodded firmly at myself in the mirror and made for the bedroom door. I bent down and picked up the chore list Darren usually put under my door and scanned it quickly. Laundry. Laundry. And, oh, more laundry.

If there was a hell, and I believed wholeheartedly that there was, it was washing and folding a never-ending pile of laundry. I didn't want to do my own, let alone that of six guys. For vampires, they sure sweated a lot. Stinky socks did not stop at human men. At least I wasn't finding some crusted over towels.

I shuddered. There wasn't enough money in the world for me to deal with that.

Making my way down the hallway and to the back stairs, I muttered to myself about the horrible unfairness that came with being the live-in maid. I couldn't call in and certainly not for cramps. That would be horrifying to explain. Besides, Darren had already sounded irritated before. We had a lot to prep for the trip, and it seemed most of it had to do with making sure the masters had enough clothes to wear.

God. Why couldn't they all just go naked? Things would be so much easier. Not to mention entertaining.

As I made my way down the back stairs, my mind started to wonder into dangerous territory.

Naked Wynn. Naked Drake and Allister. Oooh, naked Antoine. And... naked...Rayne.

My mind came to a full stop when the object of my mind's affections stood right before me in the kitchen.

He looked good. Too good. His eyes were tired, and his hair messed like he'd been running his hands through it, something my own fingers were dying to do. Like me, he wore lounge pants, but they hung low on his hips showing me the v that pointed down to his...

I swallowed thickly. Just that little expanse of skin was making me hot and bothered. Fuck.

"Uh, hi." I gave a little wave and internally groaned at how lame I sounded.

Rayne shifted away from the island where he'd been leaning and moved toward me slowly. He opened his mouth to answer me in return but then paused. A moment later, his mouth clamped shut, and his nostrils flared. I swore I heard a little rumble coming from his chest.

"Did you just... growl at me?" I eyed him suspiciously, cocking my head to the side as I tried to decipher what could be wrong.

Rayne's eyes flashed an unreadable emotion before it was gone. Instead of coming closer to me, he backed a step away.

"Uh, sorry. I..." He licked his lips. "I wanted to apologize for last night. I didn't mean to force myself on you or anything like that."

"No, no. I wanted you to kiss me." I blushed. "You didn't make me. It's just so... weird."

He huffed a laugh. "Yeah. I understand. I'm a vampire, and you're, well, you."

My lips pursed and my brows furrowed. "Hey, what's that supposed to mean?"

He shook his head as his eyes widened. "I didn't mean it like that. Just... you're not like other humans. You don't want our money. You haven't tried to jump into any of our beds."

Not outside of my head anyway.

My heart stopped, and my eyes widened as I realized what I'd just thought in front of a mind reader. I hoped against hope that he hadn't heard it, but with the way his mouth fell open and Adam's apple bobbed, that wasn't likely.

"You heard that, didn't you?" I winced as I wrung my hands together and shifted in place.

Quickly recovering, Rayne put his hands up and shook his head. "I didn't mean to. I mean, it's hard not to listen. God. Fuck! I'm messing this all up."

I let out a bitter laugh. "It's okay. Just try not to listen to hard?"

He nodded glumly.

"Good." I nodded back as the awkward tension filled the room. Not sure what else to do, I moved from the stairway and toward the coffee pot, passing closely by Rayne in the process. The only warning I had before his hand shot out and grabbed me was a deep inhale and a low curse. A blink of an eye later, I found myself pinned against the wall and Rayne's hard body, my heartbeat skyrocketing into orbit. I stared up at the redhead and gasped. "What are you doing?"

"Quiet," he commanded before dipping his head down to sniff along my neck and then my clavicle before lowering further. My body tensed and against my will, my nipples tightened. I wanted to push him away and ask what the hell he was doing, but every time I moved an inch, he let out a threatening growl.

It wasn't until his nose pushed along the edge of my shirt and pants that I stopped breathing. I knew what he was smelling. Oh, God. Why didn't I think of it before?

Because it hadn't been an issue before.

"What hadn't been?"

My head jerked down to meet Rayne's hot amber eyes. After I swallowed, I wet my lips and stuttered out, "Uh, I'm on my period."

Rayne's brows furrowed for a moment before shooting up to his forehead. The next second, he jumped back from me as if he had been burned. Stupidly, it hurt. It was a natural thing. It wasn't like I was dirty because of it. Surely, he'd been around a female while she was on her period before.

"You've been here long enough to have your period twice." Rayne seemed to come to this conclusion from somewhere. "It hasn't affected us before. What's different about now?"

I cocked my head to the side and thought about it. "Uh, well..." I fumbled with my words, not usually having to explain my body's natural actions for a man. "This time is worse than last time."

Rayne's lips turned down in a deep frown. "Is that usual?"

I shrugged. "For me. Every woman is different. Sometimes, it's barely anything, and other times..." I shrugged again like it wasn't a big deal.

Raynes thoughts were churning in his eyes, and it made me wish I was the one reading his mind. However, when he didn't say anything else, I tried to step around him and head to the coffee pot once more.

"Please don't." Rayne stopped me with his words, his feet shuffling further back the closer I got to him. I stared at him hard for a moment and then realized like a light bulb going off.

Did he want to bite me?

"No!" he cried out and then quickly lowered his voice. "It's not that... I want... Shit... please, just let me leave and then you can get your coffee."

As I watched him scramble away from me, a curious sort of feeling filled my chest. A part of me was disappointed that he hadn't stayed and done what he wanted. My traitorous vagina sure would have been on board for whatever it was he wanted to do.

"Piper! Fuck. Please stop." Rayne's jaw tightened, and his fist clenched at his sides as he paused in the doorway of the kitchen. "You don't know what you're asking."

"I didn't ask anything," I challenged him with a smirk. I was a cock tease, I knew it, but blame it on my raging hormones. My inner bitch was happy to turn the tables on him for once.

"You're thinking it." He glared at me as a rumbling growl came out of him once more. "Stop. I can't be responsible for my actions right now. Please just stop. Antoine would kill me."

"Oh?" My face lifted with amusement. I'd thought that very thing this morning. Oh, the irony. "Not if you don't tell him. I know I won't."

For a second, I thought Rayne would give into my teasing and prodding, that he'd stomp across the room and throw me down on the island before burying his face between my thighs. My lower half clenched deliciously and screamed a resounding yes to that idea.

Fate was not on our side though. Well, if Fate was named Darren. That fucking vagina blocker.

"Master Durand, can I assist you with anything?" Darren appeared behind Rayne with a tight expression on his face. He shifted between Rayne and the door frame to move into the kitchen, then eyed me before turning his attention back to Rayne.

With a half-bow, a hand to his chest, Darren asked again, "Please, let me assist you. Miss Billings has other chores to attend to."

Which was Darren's way of saying get the fuck out of the kitchen and get to work you wanton hussy. Okay, so that last part was me, but still, I could read between the lines.

"No, I'm fine. I was just going to bed." Rayne's eyes stayed locked on me the entire time, and for a moment, I think he almost gave in. Then in a blink of my eyes, he was gone.

Darren turned and scowled at me. "Why didn't you tell me you were on your menstrual cycle?"

"I didn't think it was a problem.” I shrugged. “My last cycle didn't bother them so why should this one?" I grabbed a coffee cup from the cabinet and proceeded to get my much-needed caffeine. Now, if only I could get some ice cream and hide up in my room, everything would be great.

Darren made an impatient sound in the back of his throat. "Clearly that is not the case this time. Retire to your room. You're restricted to your bedroom for the rest of the day and possibly the next three."

"What?" I shrieked as I barely kept myself from burning myself with the coffee I was pouring.

Darren marched across the kitchen and took the pot from me. Pouring my cup, he shoved the pot back into its place before giving me my cup. "You heard me. Now, while I know you cannot help when your body decides to shed its uterine lining, I expect you to be more mindful in the future of what

117

kind of household you are living in. We have enough work to do around here without you driving the masters into a frenzy."

"But what about food?" I whined, my lower lip pushing out. "I have to eat."

With a reluctant sigh, Darren lifted his eyes to the heavens. "I will bring you your meals. If there are any books you would like, I can bring those from the library for you as well. The television in your bedroom works as well if you haven't yet tried it. Now, get out of my kitchen before you end up being the next thing on the menu."

While I should have been offended by his demands of me, I just didn't have the energy to care. After all, I wanted to do exactly as he said, so before he could change his mind, I took my coffee and skipped toward the stairs. He didn't have to tell me twice.

CHAPTER 10
Wynn

I WAS WOKEN FROM a dead sleep by the most heavenly scent. Thinking it was Piper, I sat up from my bed, prepared to give her one of my devilishly wicked smiles.

"Rayne?" My smile dropped upon seeing the redhead bolt through the basement like hell was on his heels. "Why do you smell like...?" I didn't get a chance to get the words out before he slammed the door of the basement bathroom. The shower turned on next, further perturbing me.

Fully awake now, I threw my legs over the side of my bed and walked over to the shower door. I leaned against the wall and waited for Rayne to finish.

The rest of my brothers were still sound asleep. How they could be with that tantalizing scent Rayne dragged into our sanctuary was beyond me. Even Antoine who was far more observant than the rest of us had slept through it... or at least they were pretending to do so.

I had to wait a few more moments before Rayne came out of the bathroom with a towel around his waist and rubbing his wet hair with another one. He shoved his clothes into my hands with a growl.

"Burn them," he said before marching his way over to his bed.

Now that I had his clothing in my hands, the scent was even stronger. Before I could help myself, I leaned down and gave them a big sniff. Wow. That was some potent stuff.

I watched with growing amusement as he bent to retrieve the clothes he left in here for emergencies. "What's wrong with you?"

"I don't want to talk about it," Rayne grumbled as he pulled a new shirt over his head.

I held up his old clothes in my hand with a smirk. "Well, obviously it has to do with our sexy little maid or you wouldn't smell like her so." I collapsed on the bed beside him still clutching his clothes and chuckled. "Were you being naughty?"

Rayne froze, then turned his head to me where I held his clothes. "I said burn those, not rub them all over my bed." He jerked up off his bed and began stripping the sheets without waiting for me to get up.

I stood, not wanting to end up on the floor and held the clothes close to me. "Oh, I do think you were doing something utterly delicious. Tell me, did you sneak another taste?"

"No."

The bite to his voice only further amused me. I lifted the clothes to my nose once more and inhaled. With a sigh, I rubbed the fabric against my cheek. "Well, whatever you did, I've never smelled her so enticing before."

He muttered something so low that even I couldn't hear it.

"What was that?" My brows lifted and I paused in my rubbing. "I didn't quite catch it."

"She's on her period," he snapped before flinging the sheets at me. They covered my head before I could catch them in my stupefied state.

The mattress squeaked as Rayne laid down. I pulled the cover from my face and dropped it to the ground with a dry look. "What does that matter? We've been around human women on their cycles before."

"Not like this." He let out a bitter laugh. His eyes had a dark desire in them that I'd never seen on his face before. "The things I wanted to do to her..." He shuddered and hugged his arms around his chest. "What was worse were the thoughts running through her head." I arched a brow at that. "She wanted me to do those things to her, Wynn, wanted me to throw her on the island and bury my face between her thighs."

Jealousy and want flared inside of me. "Then why didn't you?"

Rayne turned his head away. "It wouldn't have been right, and besides, Darren interrupted us."

I barked a laugh. "Cockblocked by our own servant. Tragic."

"Oh, yeah. Laugh it up." Rayne waved a hand at me. "Just wait until you get a whiff. You won't be able to help yourself either."

I hummed. "Perhaps, perhaps not." I beamed at him gleefully. "However, the difference between us is I don't hold myself back. If I want something, I take it."

Rayne snorted. "That's why you haven't fucked her yet then? You must not want her very much with how much you're holding back."

My nostrils flared. "Oh, I want her. I just know patience." I eyed the clothing in my hand with a searching look. "I know a flower as delicate and temperamental as Piper has to be wooed slowly, or she'll regret it the instant it happens and will be out the door before you can get your cock out of her."

"Ugh, God, that's what I want to hear in the middle of the day." Drake groaned from his bed and rolled over to face us. "Stop talking about your dick and go to sleep. Some of us need our beauty rest."

"Forgive me from depriving you of that," I snarked back. "We all know how much you need it." A pillow came flying by my face a moment later, and I chuckled in response. "Your aim could use some improvement as well."

"Fuck off, pretty boy, and get that shit out of here before we all sprout boners." Drake flicked his hand toward the bundle in my hands. "I'd hate to be near her now based on how strong that shit is."

I stared down at the clothing and wondered if it was truly that bad or if Rayne was just being dramatic like he usually was.

"I'll be right back." I made for the door with unhurried steps, and the moment I opened the basement door, it hit me.

My cocked hardened. My fangs ached. My head moved from side to side as my nose searched out and inhaled every single delectable morsel it could. The clothing in my hand dropped to the floor without a thought, and my feet were racing through the dining room and through the kitchen, following the trail of where Piper had been last. Darren called out to me on my way through, but I ignored him. I raced up the stairs and found myself in front of Piper's bedroom.

As I breathed heavily, I leaned forward to listen. The television was on to some sitcom that had her in stitches, the laughter peeling out like tiny bells. My cheek pressed to the hardwood of her door, and I closed my eyes as I sucked in a large huff of that delicious scent.

Fuck, that was good. I let out a shuddered sigh.

Piper's laughter stopped. Her heart rate increased, and I could hear her bed creak as she stood and walked toward the door. "Who's there?"

I huffed and puffed like I was some kind of wild animal and it took me a moment to collect myself before I could get out, "It's me. Wynn."

She let out a little oh before starting toward the door, her heart beat speeding up in excitement.

"No," I snapped before she could open the door. "Don't. Don't open the door. I don't know if... Damn... Rayne was right. Please forget I was here." I spun on my heels and disappeared down the hall before her door could open.

The scent increased behind me, but I gritted my teeth and purposely put one foot in front of the other. When I slammed the basement door behind me, I took deep, cleansing, shuddering breaths.

"I told you so." Rayne smirked up at me from the bottom of the stairs. "Hard to resist, isn't she?"

"Fuck off," I snapped and shoved passed him. I closed myself in the bathroom and ignored the laughter coming from Rayne, Drake, and now apparently Allister.

As I turned the water on full heat, I didn't even bother to take my clothes off before going underneath the spray. Her scent clung to me everywhere, and I hadn't even touched her yet. Every single hair on my body stood on end while every molecule in me screamed to go back and take her. For me to soothe the aches she must be feeling, while I greedily took what I wanted from her.

I leaned my hands on the wall behind the shower head and let the water cascading over me. My hair hung in my face, clinging to my cheeks as the water soaked me through. When her scent finally dissipated, I climbed out and, with some trouble, took my wet clothes off and climbed back into the shower.

Even though her scent had waned, my cock jutted from my hips like she was there. It searched for something to penetrate and ease its throbbing. My hand wrapped around my length and gave it a long hard tug. A low groan escaped me, and I closed my eyes.

God. Fuck. Piper.

In my mind, I hadn't stopped her from opening the door. Piper stood there, clad in a pair of those tiny pajama shorts she walked around in when she thought no one was around. Her breasts were bare beneath her thin tank top, her nipples straining against the fabric as they yearned for me to take them into my mouth.

I pulled on my cock even faster now. My breaths came in pants as I pictured taking her in my arms. My hands would cup that deliciously round ass as I jerked her to my front, grinding my cock into her stomach so she could see how much she affected me.

"Wynn!" she'd cry out as she leaned her head back, her lips poised and ready for me to take. And I would have. I'd have kissed her until she felt it all the way down in her toes, until she begged me to take her to her bed and make sweet, sweet love to her.

I wanted to drive myself inside of her until she gripped me so tightly, she never wanted me to leave. And I would. I promised myself as I released all over the side of the shower wall that I'd have her. If she became bound to us, I'd have all of eternity to have her beneath me and every other way I wanted her.

A banging on the bathroom door made me turn the shower off and climb out. I grabbed a towel from the rack and opened the door to reveal a smirking Rayne.

"Have a good wank?"

"Bugger off." I shoved past him and climbed into my bed, wet hair and towel and all. Folding my arms over my chest, I closed my eyes and tried to drown them out, but my brothers were persistent. I should have known better than to think I could ignore them.

"Man," Allister whistled, "if the great Wynn couldn't hold his own without a good tugging on the flag pool then I'm scared to even step foot out of the basement."

Drake and Allister chuckled.

"I think it would be a good time as any to go to the club," Drake proclaimed.

I cracked an eye open at that. He and Allister sat side by side on Drake's bed, grinning like they were having the best time of their undead lives.

Twats.

"What do you say, Wynn?" Drake paused in his conversation with Allister to arch a brow at me. "Want to come with us? Wet your whistle and your dick?"

Rayne scoffed and rolled his eyes. He'd never been one for the exclusive club that we sometimes frequented at in Atlanta. Said it was too easy. I had to agree with him in some ways, but to me, the biggest challenge was getting a woman who did it for the money to decline payment.

There was no bigger thrill, and I'd had a few of my own over the centuries.

"Sure," I muttered as I closed my eyes once more. "I'll come, but we'll have to wait until dark. I don't want to run into Piper."

Rayne laughed bitterly. "Oh, yes. Don't want our precious maid to know what despicable deviants we are." He snorted a laugh. "Not like she doesn't know already."

My eyes opened into slits, watching our younger brother scowl. He really needed a good wank.

"Go jerk off before your bad mood rubs off on us." Drake jerked his arms in front of him before smoothing his hands over the sides of his buzzed head. "I don't want it stinking me up for the ladies."

I smiled to myself. Sometimes we were so in sync I didn't even have to say what I thought, my brothers did it for me. Regardless, I thought really hard about Piper's breasts, recreating the fantasy I had in the shower before shoving it at Rayne.

To my satisfaction, he sucked in a breath and shot those amber eyes my way. "Real mature."

I lifted a shoulder. Somethings time didn't change.

CHAPTER 11
Piper

I WAS LOUNGING AROUND in my pajamas one evening when I realized I needed a drink. My mouth felt like it was full of cotton balls, and I was desperate for something other than water.

But it was after six o'clock. The masters were up, and Darren would be bringing my dinner any time now. Again.

Three days. I'd been stuck in my room for three days. In theory, being waited on hand

and foot was a wish come true, but in reality? It sucked hairy man balls.

I couldn't leave my room. I'd call Darren but he and the rest of the house seem to be allergic to answering the phone. That or it was just when I called. I tried texting him my request but all that got me was a rude glare and cold pasta for dinner.

Besides being thirsty, I was bored. I'd read all the books I wanted to, watched as much mindless television as I possibly could, but I needed human interaction. More importantly, my period body had shifted into its inevitable horny mood and wanted nothing more than to hop on the first vampire I saw for some relief.

But that wasn't the worst of it. That was reserved for the dreams. I already had pretty vivid dreams about the masters as it was, but this time, my period really must be yearning for the relief the vampires could give me whether or not my mind kind of found the thought icky.

I refused to touch myself though.

Antoine's words and the thought of them hearing me was more than enough of a deterrent to cool my raging libido. Even when I was in the bathtub and wanted nothing more than to throw my head back against the rim and go to town on myself, I didn't trust the horny bitch inside of me not to moan.

Even now, sitting here on my bed and staring holes in my door as I willed Darren to hurry up with my dinner, I wanted nothing more than to slip my hand into my pants or at least grind against my clit to stop the constant ache.

"Screw it," I declared as I jumped off my bed. I marched toward the door and hesitated only for a moment before pulling the door open. I was sort of surprised that it wasn't locked. Darren had been pretty adamant about me staying in my room. I guess he trusted me to keep my word, a horrible decision on his part really.

I popped my head out into the hallway and searched for the grumpy butler. No sign of him. With a skip and a grin, I stepped into the hallway and closed my bedroom door behind me. My night shorts did nothing to shelter me against the chill of the hallway. I shivered and rubbed my hands over my bare arms, wishing I'd at least worn something other than a tank top.

Hey, at least I was wearing a bra. That counted for something, right?

As I made my way to the kitchen, I frowned. It was quiet, too quiet for after six o'clock. The masters were usually up and about causing all kinds of mayhem or having some kind of dinner party I wasn't allowed to attend because they didn't want to scar my delicate sensibilities.

I snorted and rolled my eyes.

Delicate, my ass.

I wasn't stupid. I knew they hired women to drink from. It wasn't like I was going to stop them or try to save the women. They were getting paid after all. They got paid to cuddle up to Wynn, to put their hands in his hair as he pressed opened mouth kisses to their neck before letting his fangs slip inside of them.

A pang of jealousy made me rub my chest.

Stop it. They aren't yours. You can't get mad that they're feeding on them and not you. Besides, you don't want them to bite you, do you?

Well, to be honest, maybe I was a bit curious. I mean, who wouldn't be? I lived with six sexy as hell vampires who hadn't so much as hinted at biting me. Rayne had nicked me with his fangs the first time we kissed, but that was about it. I was disappointed that they had such self-control around me.

Call me crazy, but shouldn't the men I like have a hard time controlling themselves around me?

I shook my head at the thought as I came into the kitchen. No one was there either, not even Darren. I frowned.

Where was everyone?

Desperate for attention but also dying for a drink, I went to the fridge first to quench my thirst. Inside, I found a soda and also a crap ton of bottles of blood. With a curious look at the bottles, I glanced around the kitchen as if I expected someone to come in and reprimand me. When no one did, I picked up one of the silver metal containers and twisted the cap off. I bent my nose against the rim and sniffed.

My nose crinkled in disgust as the coppery metal smell hit my nose. I quickly closed the lid and put it back before shutting the fridge door. As I did, it revealed that Darren now stood on the other side of it.

"Jesus, Mary, and Joseph!" I grabbed my chest and breathed heavily as I glared at the stoic butler. "What the hell are you doing, sneaking around in a vampire's lair?"

I had to give it to Darren, his lips didn't even so much as twitch. Instead, his eyes had even more condescension in them than usual. "Are you done?"

After staring at him for a moment, I didn't know what he was talking about them and then it dawned on me. "No. Not yet."

"Then you shouldn't be out of your room."
His voice was sharp and almost hurtful but I
brushed it aside.

"I was thirsty." I showed him my can of
soda.

Darren shook his head grimly and moved
to the counter where the dinner tray he had
started for me sat. "Which could have waited
five more minutes. What would you have
done had the masters been having dinner?"

"Well, I—"

"When all six of them caught your scent
and closed in on you before you could even
realize your folly? What then?" he bit out,
never once looking at me as he arranged the
plates and napkins on my tray.

"I'm sorry, I didn't mean—"

"Of course, you didn't," he cut me off
again, flicking his eyes up to me before they
moved back down to the tray. He went about
folding and refolding the cloth napkin with
jerky gestures. "You never do."

"Hey, now wait a second," I objected.
"That's hardly fair."

"Isn't it though?" He paused and stared
hard at me, making me squirm in place. "You
prance around here in those little shorts and
barely there tops and then get surprised
when the masters react to you." He huffed a
bitter laugh. "They all think you are different

because you haven't climbed into bed with them or flat-out propositioned them, but you're worse. You're the worst kind of seducer because you don't even try, and they fall all over themselves to have you."

Darren stopped for a moment and then his jaw tightened. "Mark my words, have you they will, and then they won't want to let you go."

I gaped at him, opening and closing my mouth like a codfish as I stood there in the kitchen. My quickly warming soda was in one hand, and my beating heart had been ripped out and now sat on the island for Darren to smash.

I forced my mouth shut and narrowed my eyes on him. "I don't know what your problem is today, but I am not trying to do anything."

"My point exactly—" he tried to interject, but I was having no part of it.

"Stop it. I'm talking now." I held my hand up with a warning glare. "I understand you have a special relationship with the masters, but I'm here now too. I don't want to take them away from you or anything like that. I just wanted a job, and they gave me one."

"You could get another job," he quipped.

"Not like this one." I shook my head. "Not one where I actually feel like I belong and have a place. At least I did, until you basically called me a sneaky whore," I growled, but Darren didn't even act contrite.

"I admit I'm attracted to them." I shrugged. "Who wouldn't be? But I'm not just going to ruin our whole dynamic just to get my rocks off. So, you can take your condescending attitude and shove it up your ass where the rest of your personality lives." I huffed and spun on my heel marching toward the stairs. Then I stopped and spun back around.

"And another thing! I don't parade around in my pajamas. I didn't expect to run into any of them." I waved my hand around the kitchen. "Obviously, no one is even home. So... yeah... there," I ended lamely with a wince.

Darren sighed and shook his head. "They aren't here because they can't stand to be in the same house as you right now. Even with you locked in your room, they are going mad with bloodlust with just the faintest whiff of you."

My brows shot up to my forehead at his words. Was my period really affecting them so much? I swallowed hard, my heart suddenly beating rapidly against my chest as I squeaked out, "All of them?"

"All of them what?"

"All of them are mad with... with... bloodlust?" It felt weird to even say it, but I had to know who to keep away from until my cycle subsided.

Darren nodded. "Yes. Now if you would go back to your room, I'll have dinner ready in a moment. Better to keep your scent in one place as much as possible."

My irritation had been replaced by unease as I made my way back upstairs to my room. I hated to think I was causing the masters problems. I mean, how could my scent be so bad that they had to leave the house? I paused in the hallway and gave my armpit a sniff. I didn't smell anything other than my deodorant. Then again, I didn't have supernatural senses. The only time I'd been able to smell more than usual was that one-time Wynn gave me his blood. If I'd had some of that, maybe I'd get what the big deal was, but oh well.

With a sigh, I went to my bedroom door, but before I could enter, a presence made me pause. I slowly turned and met the heavy gaze of Antoine standing in the middle of the hallway. Dressed in a grey business suit that clung to him like it was bespoke, he wore his long blonde hair down so that it brushed the shoulders of his jacket. One hand was tucked into the pocket of his slacks, and the other lifted the slate blue tie around his neck. I caught myself staring at him longer than I meant to before quickly closing my mouth as I licked my lips.

"Uh, hey. I thought you were gone with the others?"

"I had business to attend to." His voice was tight and low, almost a growl that made my insides twist wantonly. His pale blue eyes were dark with a mixture of pain and hunger. It made me freeze in place, too afraid to run in fear that he would chase me.

"Oh," I breathed and then slowly pointed to my door. "I was just going back to my room. Don't mind me."

A warning growl stopped me from turning the door handle. My eyes shot back to him wide with a mixture of fear and... desire? So weird. I never thought I was the kind of woman who liked a man growling like an animal at her, but here I was, soaking wet for Antoine.

"Master Durand..." My voice cracked. I swallowed and then tried again. "I think I should leave."

He took a step toward me and then stopped and shook his head. His eyes lifted back up to mine. "Antoine."

"Uh... what?"

"Call me Antoine."

If possible, my arousal spiked even higher. What the actual fuck?

Gasping for breath, I nodded. "Okay, Antoine. I think I should go into my room."

"You should," he agreed, but neither of us moved for me to do just that.

"Yeah. I—"

Without warning, Antoine turned his back to me and started down the hallway. Just when I thought he had forgotten me, he called over his shoulder. "Come."

CHAPTER 12
Antoine

AT FIRST, PIPER DIDN'T move away from the door, her mouth ajar as she stared at me in disbelief. I was quickly learning her different expressions. She didn't have many.

A little shaky smile when she was nervous. A broad grin when she was particularly pleased with something. When she was annoyed, her brows would furrow between her eyes before anger took over, making her nostrils flare out and her teeth gnash together. However, the best expression was when she was aroused.

Her small tongue would dart out of her tempting mouth, sliding along her lower lip before a soft sigh would release from her throat. It was accompanied with her thighs pressing together tightly as she tried to stifle the pulsating need ripping through her lower regions.

It was a reaction I had only witnessed once or twice, but right now, with the overwhelming scent of her cycle filling my very senses, I wanted nothing more than to cause that reaction in her.

"Miss Billings." My voice held a firm authority I used with my brothers as I waited for her to follow my instructions. "Do not make me repeat myself."

Her heartbeat fluttered, but then the telltale sound of her small feet padded across the hallway floor as she hurried to follow me. I didn't know why I told her to come, but the words were out of my mouth before I could stop myself, and I was never one to retract what has already been said.

I brought her to my office and held the door open for her as she walked past me, trying not to touch me as she did. It was laughable how tense she was. It was not me she should fear, but my brothers.

I followed her and closed the door behind me. She stood in the middle of my office, her hands fidgeting in front of her short shorts. Those shorts that hugged her backside so delectably, it was as if they were poured onto her skin. My fingers ached to cup those glorious globes and hear the little gasp that would come from her when I did so.

"What's up?" Piper glanced nervously toward me as I rounded my desk, my fingers trailing along the top of the wood surface.

I let the silence permeate the room until Piper's brows furrowed. My lips tipped up at the annoyance filling her. "It has come to my attention that you have little regard for your wellbeing or those of this household."

Her lips parted as her eyes widened and her heartbeat tripled in speed. "What?" Her throat bobbed as she swallowed. "What do you mean?"

Instead of taking my seat, I rounded the desk once more and sat on the edge of my desk, hands sitting in my lap as I surveyed her. Yes, my presence was causing her more distress the closer I came. As I locked my eyes on her panicked brown ones, I held back a smirk. Instead, I set my lips into a firm line. "Miss Billings, what am I?"

Her lips twisted in a frown as her brows bunched adorably in confusion. "Uh… really tall?"

Not letting myself sigh in frustration, I urged her on. "What else?"

Her eyes slid over my form, from the bottom of my tailored shoes to my custom suit her, scent growing more intense as her gaze roamed. When her eyes finally settled on my face, she wet her lips and parted her lips once more. "A vampire."

I nodded, pleased with her answer. "And what do vampires eat?"

Piper's face flushed as she breathed out, "Blood."

I crossed my arms over my chest and settled a knowing look on her. "And do you think that teasing a vampire while you are in your current condition is a wise decision?"

Confusion covered her face for a brief moment before her eyes widened a fraction and her mouth dropped open. Instead of recoiling in fear like a good human facing on a blood-sucking immortal, her face flashed with anger. Her nostrils flared, and her eyes lit with a fire I'd only seen a few times.

If I hadn't already been hard as a rock, I would have been now.

"Well, excuse me," she started before standing to her feet. "I wasn't aware that my bodily functions, ones I can't control, were such a hindrance to you." She scoffed, crossed her arms over her chest, pushing her already tempting breasts up further, and tapped her foot on the floor incessantly. "You know, this is really ridiculous. If you can't handle a female having her period, then you shouldn't hire one to clean your house. It's common sense."

If anyone else had talked to me in such a manner, I would have put them down right then and there. I hadn't gotten to where I was now by being nice. I'd gotten it with bloodshed and power. Over the years, as I cultivated my abilities and reputation, there had been considerably less bloodshed because those below me knew better than to challenge me.

Except for this one, this little human female who glared at me like I was the scum beneath her foot and I should be the one so lucky to speak to her, let alone have her as my employee. It made me want to laugh, rage, and kiss her all at once. I'd never felt such conflicting feelings for someone, not even when I was a human myself.

I dropped my arms and took a step toward her. She flinched and stepped back, a flash of worry in her eyes. At least, I knew she wasn't stupid, just too brave for her own tiny britches.

"Miss Billings," I began and then caught sight of her tongue wetting her lips again. "Piper." I took another step.

She stood her ground this time, her chin up high and her little hands clenched into fists like a child preparing to have a temper tantrum.

As I stopped before her, I reached a hand out and cupped the side of her face. Her eyes widened slightly, and her heart rate kicked up a notch. Arousal and the sweet tang of her blood permeated the air, and it took everything I had not to turn her around and bend her over my desk right then and there.

"Antoine?" she murmured back, almost as if she weren't sure of herself or my intentions.

Not that I'd given her any idea of what was going on inside of my head. I scarcely knew that right now either. My hand slid around to grasp the back of her neck, making a small pained noise escape from her lips. I held her firmly, but not hard enough to hurt her, then arched her head back to meet my gaze.

"We are vampires, Piper. Whether or not you can control what your body does, you should be aware that we are not human men." I lowered my face, brushing my nose

146

against the side of her face as I inhaled deeply. Her body stiffened as I pressed myself against her. When she felt the length of my arousal against her stomach, she let out a startled gasp but didn't push me away. If anything, her own arousal spiked even more.

Encouraged by her response, I trailed my nose along her jawline and then down the side of her neck. Her heart rate kicked up in response, and I could feel the tension in her. She wanted it but was afraid at the same time. It made the scent of her blood even more delicious. My fangs ached to pierce her milky white flesh and taste her on my tongue.

A part of me was jealous of Rayne for getting to her first. It was that part that allowed me to open my mouth and tease her with the tips of my fangs, not biting down but letting her know they were there. Her hands reached up from where they had been motionless at her sides and landed on my chest, but she didn't push me away or pull me closer. They just sat there as if she were still debating her reaction.

Once again, I felt jealous of Rayne. Oh, to see inside of her head right now.

To distract myself from taking what I wanted, I murmured against her skin, "Perhaps you mean to torture us. Do you mean to bring out the monster in us? Are we that unbearable to work for?"

Her throat moved beneath my mouth as she swallowed hard and stuttered, "N...no. I like it here."

"What is it then?" My other arm wrapped around her waist and held her tightly to my chest as her hands on my chest twisted into my shirt. "Do you wish for us to take you? Do you want to know the sting of my kiss against your neck as I feed on you? Is that it?"

Piper didn't answer, but that was enough, to begin with. She wanted something from us, whether she wanted to admit it or not.

I was about to give it to her before a knock sounded on my door, breaking the spell between us. Piper shoved against my chest, and I stepped back as I abruptly released her. I adjusted my tie and turned my back on her as I waved toward the door.

"Go to your room and don't come back out until it's done. Next time I won't be so lenient."

As I rounded my desk and sat down, I didn't meet her eyes, but I could hear the outrage in her voice as she bit out, "Of course, master. Whatever you wish." Out of the corner of my eye, she mock-curtsied before marching out over to the door and swinging it open.

Darren stood on the other side with a blank expression on his face. I knew my servant well enough to know he was not happy with something. I also knew he would tell me as soon as he was ready.

Piper flicked her gaze toward me and then back to Darren. "Maybe you can help our master pry the stick out of his ass. He seems to have gotten one lodged up there somewhere."

Darren's brows lifted a fraction to break his poker face briefly. Piper stomped away without another word and left us alone in the office. I lifted my hand and quirked two fingers at him, and Darren moved into the office.

"Close the door."

I didn't have to tell him why, Darren just did it. How refreshing it was for one of my employees to actually obey my orders. However, Darren had several lifetimes to get used to my commands, and I knew part of him liked doing what I asked, even more so than being in charge of my entire household. The man always had a thing for order. From his ebony hair slicked back without a hair out of place to the freshly pressed suit he wore on his sinewy frame, Darren was nothing but orderly, tight down to the pristine white gloves covering his hands.

No, Darren was the perfect servant in every way. He always knew what I needed and was happy to give it to me, and right now, I needed a release.

Without having to ask, Darren moved around the desk and knelt in front of me. His hands reached for my pants, but I pushed them away. I gestured for him to stand up. As he moved back to his feet, Darren waited for my command.

"I am yours, whatever you need." Darren's eyes locked with mine as he repeated the same words he'd said to me so long ago when we were in a similar position. I needed something, and he gave it to me, regardless of what it was.

Some might find our relationship twisted, sick, but it worked for us. Darren had been dying, and when I had saved him all those years ago, I didn't use that salvation as a bargaining chip or leverage over him. No, his servitude was at a mutual benefit. I needed someone I could trust with my life and that of my brothers, to be the eyes and ears during the day time when we could not be, and while our relationship had not started out physical, it had become that and more

150

when he had offered himself to me much like he was now.

"Turn around." I moved my chair away from the desk and stood, allowing him to take my place. When he was in front of me, I commanded, "Bend over."

Without a word, he unbuttoned his slacks and dropped them to the ground before bending at the waist before me. My eyes swept over the pale skin revealed to me my already hard cock dripping and ready for release. I unbuckled my belt with one hand and reached into the drawer of my desk for a small bottle of lube. I released my cock from my pants and squirted some of the cool gel onto it. As I wrapped my hand around myself, I gave it a few good tugs before moving closer to Darren.

Darren let out a low grunt as I pushed inside of him, one of my hands on his back and the other on his hip as I moved. His fingers curled around the edges of my desk, the knuckles turning white as he let out little gasps and groans before I grabbed that perfectly slicked back hair and gave it a good tug. That made him cry out and release on the floor beneath my desk. I was not too far behind him, letting out my own grunt of pleasure as I finished.

As I pulled out, I gave Darren a slight pat on his bare butt before moving back. He quickly stood and grabbed the handkerchief from his pocket, cleaning himself off before turning to do the same to me. Once he was done, I redid my pants and moved around the room while he cleaned the mess on the floor.

"Have the others all gone to the club?" I picked up my cell phone from the desk and looked at my messages. None of my brothers had messaged me, but that wasn't surprising. They didn't have to tell me every single aspect of their life, not like our sire would have required. It was part of the reason we became our own house.

"Yes," Darren answered and stood. He smoothed his hand over his head, trying to smooth the hair I had tousled. "They left as soon as the sun set."

"Good." I nodded and waited for the reason Darren had come to my office in the first place.

"The preparations for this weekend are completed," he reported, "though it was slow going because of unforeseeable consequences."

I snorted. Unforeseeable consequences, indeed. "And how is our little maid doing? She is easily frazzled." I let out a rare chuckle. "I almost thought she would hit me just now."

Darren's lips twitched. "Piper is of a different breed that is for certain." The humor on his face disappeared, and a more serious expression took its place. "Speaking of which, this weekend has me concerned."

"About?"

"Miss Billings and the interest Valentine has in her."

I inclined my head. "Yes, I am aware. We hope to rectify that by binding her to us."

Darren's brows furrowed at my words. "I'm not certain that will work the way you hope. There have been other developments that I have implored Piper to bring to your attention, but she has not heeded my request."

I looked up from my phone and quirked a brow. "Such as?"

Darren seemed uncomfortable, an unusual feat for him. "Ever since Valentine visited, a bouquet of flowers has been delivered every day to Miss Billings." He paused as if he didn't want to tell me. "From Valentine."

My brows shot up to my forehead. "Really? And these flowers, were they accompanied by messages, or were they just signed by the bastard?"

"Yes," Darren breathed out, clearly happy to finally have the secret off of his chest. "The notes he has sent are similar to those we'd seen back in Prague."

My eyes narrowed, and my lips pressed into a thin line, a low growl coming from my throat before I could stop it. "No more flowers. I don't care if you have to bar all deliveries to the house. He will not turn Piper into Danielle. I won't stand for it."

Darren nodded his head. "It will be done."

I turned back to my phone as Darren left the room. The tension I'd just gotten rid of had come back with a vengeance. Valentine was the worst kind of predator, the kind that took pleasure in tormenting and torturing his prey before finally putting them out of their misery. However, he liked to hide the fact that he was even hunting you behind gifts and pleasant smiles. His victims rarely knew they were being hunted until it was too late. Thankfully, Piper had us to protect her.

Danielle DePuff had not been so lucky.

CHAPTER 13
Marcus

THE VIPER CLUB WAS a kind of sticky warm that made you want to take a shower just to get the stink off. Unfortunately, it was the closest vampire club to us which only gives us so many options. I'd have much preferred hunting down my prey for the evening, but the others... needed an easy release, especially after the maid kept prancing around the house like she wasn't a beacon for vampires everywhere.

Here, at least, we had a slight reprieve. The Viper Club was all hard lines and shiny surfaces. Even the lighting in here was harsh, washing out our otherwise already pale skin even more, but the couches were the worst part.

Made of some slick, rubbery material, they were scattered around the place in reds and white. For a place that caters to vampires, they sure didn't know what a vampire liked. Most vampires, including myself, were several centuries old. We were used to more lavish, decorative places that strived for comfort than edginess.

I shook my head. This generation.

"Fuck." My head turned as Drake drew out the word. A blonde woman ground against his lap, dressed in only a lacy black thong. His head thrown back and his eyes closed, he gripped her hips tightly with both hands. "Darling, you're going to have me bursting all over my nice jeans."

The blonde simply grinned coquettishly and ground harder, tossing her hair over her shoulder as she offered him her neck. Drake wasted no time sinking his fangs into the woman, and both of them groaned in satisfaction.

I turned my gaze from Drake to the rest of my brothers. Allister was in much the same position as his with twin a woman in his lap and his fangs in her neck. The difference was that his eyes weren't closed, they were staring off at nothing as if he imagined something else entirely in his head. Wynn had three women around him, one on each arm and another rubbing his shoulders. The one behind him played with his hair as he took turns biting each woman, all bare-chested and rubbing up against him like cats in heat.

Without Antoine here, the others really let loose, all except... Rayne. He had yet to take a woman for blood or sex as far as I could tell. Instead, he took up residence at the bar the moment we arrived and hadn't moved an inch. The mind reader scanned the room over his glass of scotch and scowled.

I wondered what he heard that put him in such a bad mood.

Drake let out a grunt as the woman a sighed, causing my head to turn toward them once more. He pulled back with a drunken grin and patted the woman on the butt before gently pushing her off his lap. "Thanks, darling."

We didn't need to pay the women it was included in the club's yearly fee, a substantial amount of more than ten grand per vampire. The women were paid handsomely for it, and from what I could tell, the majority of them enjoyed every second of it.

"Better?" I arched a brow at Drake.

He ran his thumb along his lower lip with a smile. "Much." His eyes flickered from me to Rayne, and he jerked his head at our brother. "What's up with him?"

I shrugged cluelessly.

"Have you eaten?" Drake asked as he turned his eyes away from Rayne, our little brother forgotten for the moment. "I can call her back if you...?"

I held my hand up and shook my head. "No."

Allister pulled back from his date long enough to quip, "Marcus doesn't do paid meals, you know that. He likes the thrill of the hunt." He winked at me, and I resisted the urge to roll my eyes as he went back to his date. She let out a long breathy moan as his fangs sunk into her once more.

"Hunting is great and everything," Drake began as he leaned forward to pick up his beer before taking a swig. "But why make things harder than they have to be? They're bought and paid for." He swept a hand around the room at the other gorgeous woman, all in various stages of undress.

"Why not take pleasure from them, if not blood?"

I snorted and shifted in my seat. I crossed my arms over my chest and lifted my chin. "Only a truly hopeless man has to pay for his meal or his love."

"Oh, but what fun it is." Wynn looked up from the breasts of one of his companions. He smirked and eyed me as he cupped her breasts, thumb tracing the outline of her already hardened nipple. The woman, another blonde, I was beginning to see a trend, arched into his touch and panted lustily. The room stunk with sex and blood, more the former than the latter.

Vampires were neat eaters for the most part as long as we weren't trying to be cruel. There was no need to spill more blood than needed. It was wasteful, and if my brothers and I were anything, we weren't wasteful.

"Are you worried?" Drake asked, crossing one leg over the other as he leaned back against the couch. "About the summons?"

"Of course."

Only an idiot or a fool wouldn't be worried. Being summoned was not something to be taken lightly, especially since we were taking an unbound human with us. It was a complication we didn't need.

"Are you more worried about what our sire wants or our little maid?" Wynn lazily licked his lips as he switched from the blonde to her brunette friend on his other side. She freely offered her neck to him, but he grinned wickedly at her before pushing her back to lie on the couch. As he leaned over her, he lifted one tanned thigh up before biting into her [vein] artery. The woman gasped one hand going to the back of his head while the other grabbed at the rubbery couch for a handhold, of which there were none.

"He doesn't give two shits about our maid," Rayne answered for me. He had finally left the safety of the bar and come over to stand by our group.

"He'd rather us wipe her and dump her somewhere. She's a complication," he mimicked my thoughts with a sneer.

I didn't even bother to defend myself. I did believe that. Rayne had read it from my mind, and there was no point of arguing it.

"Ah, come on," Drake scoffed and shook his glass, letting the ice tinkle against the sides. "You can't be that cold-hearted. Don't tell me not a single part of you wants to keep her around? Even just for the thrill of the chase?" He arched a brow at me, and I tightened my jaw, my lips in a flat line.

"Don't bother." Allister shook his head as one hand stroked the shoulder of his companion lovingly. "Marcus only has a heart for politics, and Piper can only be seen as a weakness."

"A fucking hot-as-hell weakness." Drake barked a laugh and was quickly joined by his brother. Wynn made a grunt of acknowledgment, but he was otherwise occupied.

Rayne, however, had much to say. "Well, whatever she is, her being on her... cycle..." His eyes flared hot as he said it before he took several breaths and contained himself. "... while at the sire's will put a dent in all of our armors. Let's hope that she finishes before Friday."

"Perhaps someone should help her out?" Allister arched a brow and then cupped the chin on the woman in his lap. "Hurry the process along. I've read that intercourse really speeds up the process. Isn't that right, love?" He nipped at her mouth, and she eagerly agreed.

"Well," Drake sat down his glass on the table in front of us and stood. He held his hand up with a lopsided grin. "I volunteer as tribute."

Rayne let out a low growl. "The fuck you do. If anyone's going to speed up the process, it's me."

Wynn took a moment to lift his head from his companion who had quite literally passed out from pleasure. "Listen to little brother. He was the first to taste her and now he thinks he owns her." His eyes crinkled at the edges as he pulled a handkerchief from his pocket. As he wiped a bit of blood from the corner of his mouth, he winked. "I'd love to ask Piper what she thinks of that."

Rayne took a step forward, his fingers curled into tight fists. "Fuck you. Unlike you, I don't need to use my powers to attract someone."

Drake snorted. "No, you just read their mind, find out what they like, then exploit it. That's what you did with Piper, didn't you?"

Rayne flushed red and snapped. "You don't know what you're talking about. It doesn't work that way. I can't just dig into her head at will. She has to be thinking about it already. You know that!"

"Still, you can't say that you haven't used your abilities to get ahead with Piper." Allister pointed an accusing finger at Rayne. "You're not as innocent as you think you are."

"I didn't say that I was, but still, I've made more headway than any of you." Rayne gritted his teeth and crossed his arms over his chest. "Do you really think she'd accept it from someone she hasn't even kissed yet?" His face finally relaxed as he grinned smugly at them. "I've kissed her twice. How many times have you?"

There was silence around the room, and then Wynn spoke up. "Once... and let's not forget that first kiss of yours was forced on by Valentine, so it doesn't count." His lips tipped at the edges. "So, I believe that makes us even."

Rayne's face scrunched up with annoyance before he gestured toward the three women with a nasty laugh. "Not for long when I tell her what you've spent all day doing."

"You will do no such thing." We all turned at the sound of Antoine's voice to see him standing behind us. A waitress brought him a drink, and he nodded his thanks before moving toward us. "What happens in the club stays here. You know the rules."

Rayne flinched at Antoine's commanding voice but nodded.

"As for Piper," he continued as he took the seat next between Drake and me, "I suggest we focus on binding her to our house instead of fighting over who will bed her first."

A woman passed by and gave Antoine a once over, and he quirked a finger in her direction. She happily complied, stalking over to him on four-inch spike heels. She had long light brown hair, big brown eyes, and an innocent air that reminded me of our maid.

I resisted the urge to huff. Even our leader was obsessed with the human woman.

"She'll bind to us," Wynn announced as he took a break from his debauchery to drink deeply from his wine glass. "There's nothing to fear in that area."

Antoine frowned and cocked his head to the side. "What makes you so confident?"

Wynn twirled the wine glass in between his fingers and looked at Antoine with hooded lids. "Piper's curious by nature. She can't help it. Piper will want to know what the big fuss is about, and she's too attracted to the lot of us to give it all up now. Trust me." He sighed and leaned back into the women's arms. "She'll be more than willing to bind herself to our house, even more so if I'm the one to do it."

Wynn's words sparked a whole other argument between my brothers. They really were a ridiculous lot. Who loses their head over a human?

I was thankful to be safely immune to her charms.

CHAPTER 14
Piper

AS SOON AS THE sun set on one of the last days of my period, I found myself creeping over to my bedroom door, pressing my ear to it as I listened for any sound of the masters. Sadly, they were quieter than most human men. I barely could hear voices, let alone footsteps when they went by.

I almost opened the door one time when I thought one of them had stopped outside of it. My hand sat on the door handle, my face shoved against the door, listening and waiting to see what they would do. When they didn't seem to make any kind of move to knock on my door, I found my hand turning the knob. Irritatingly enough, the moment I pulled the door open, they were gone without even a whiff of them left behind.

Boredom aside, I was lonely. I wanted some kind of interaction. Human, vampire, anything. Darren still brought my meals to my room, but he only ever stayed around for a few moments before disappearing to do God only knew what in the rest of the house, probably doing my chores along with his own.

A part of me was guilty about making him do my work while I still got paid for it, but then I remembered it was him who made me stay in time-out and then demanded I get over it.

Oh well, only a few more hours and I'll be home free.

I sighed and clicked the remote at the TV as I turned it off and stood. I'd taken to wearing my pajamas all the time because no one else was going to see me. I'd walk around in just my underwear if I weren't hyper-aware of the masters being close by. Part of me hoped they would come knock on my door, and then I'd have a reason to talk to them. The other part remembered how Rayne had reacted in the kitchen.

I shivered on my way to the bathroom.

It had been exhilarating and frightening all at once. One, to know that the redhead was that affected by my blood to have to restrain himself so much. Two, the hot need in his eyes made my own body heat up and slick with desire. Three, if I let him bite me would he be able to stop? Antoine had done a good job of reminding me of just how dangerous they could be, and while it was arousing to think of them getting out of control with me, it was also a completely horrible idea.

With that in mind, I went about brushing my teeth and letting out small sighs of despair. I looked in the mirror and snorted. Wasn't I a sight? My blonde hair was pulled up in a messy bun, but since I hadn't bothered fixing it up today, it was lopsided and falling out. My eyes were dull from too much sleep, and I was pretty sure my clothes were the same ones I'd worn two days ago... or were they?

I didn't know. The days had blurred together so that I no longer even bothered to look at the clock. I only remembered to look at what time it was when Darren brought me my food. Which he should be doing any minute now.

I finished brushing my teeth, spat, and rinsed. Unable to handle my disgusting hair any longer, I decided to jump in the shower. I turned the water on until it scorched my skin and just stood under the spray. The water pounded against my shoulders, loosening up the muscles there, and I tipped my head back to let it soak into my hair. Then, after pouring a generous amount of shampoo in my hand, I began to scrub my hair vigorously.

Halfway through scrubbing, there was a knock on the door. My head jerked up which caused soap to get in my eyes. Wincing in pain, I shouted, "Come in," as I tried to get the soap out of my eyes. I rubbed and whimpered at the stinging pain. The door opened and closed in the other room. "Just put the tray on the table. I'll be out in a second, I want to talk to you."

I grabbed the loofa and quickly scrubbed my body as I didn't want to keep Darren waiting. Yes, I was that desperate for someone to talk to.

"I wasn't aware you missed me that much."

Wynn's voice startled me. I grabbed for the shower curtain, only intending to peek around the corner of it to be sure I'd heard him right. However, the curtain wasn't that sturdy, and just then, my foot slipped on the soapy bottom of the tub. I held on for dear life as I put all my weight on the curtain... and that's when it tore free from the curtain rod. With a banshee-like wail, I went flying out of the bathtub and toward the hard tile floor of the bathroom.

Quick as lightning, Wynn was at my side. His arms wrapped around me and the shower curtain, keeping me from breaking my head open on the floor.

I gasped and stared up at him. "Uh, thanks."

"You're welcome." Wynn's lips curled into an amused grin as his blue eyes twinkled down at me. "You really shouldn't keep your bedroom door unlocked. Anyone could just walk in."

I frowned. "I thought you were Darren."

Wynn brushed the hair out of my face, and his eyes moved down over my very wet and very exposed naked body. "Lucky him."

My body warmed as I struggled against his hold, reaching for my towel in the process. Wynn smirked and didn't even bother pretending like he wasn't checking me out as I escaped his grasp, stumbling as

I clutched my towel. The desire in his eyes was obvious as well as the bulge in his pants.

Now with a few feet between us, I shoved my hair behind my ears, holding my towel around me tightly as I searched for something to say. "I thought you were all spending the week at the club?"

I didn't know much about the club Darren claimed the masters were spending their week at. I'd tried to look it up online, but the website for The Viper had been sparse for information with only their logo and a phone number and address. If I had been braver, I'd have driven up to Atlanta myself and checked it out. However, since it was a vampire club and I have already grounded to my bedroom because of my period, the smarter part of me decided this would just be one mystery they kept to themselves.

"I was." Wynn leaned against the bathroom door, his gaze moving from my body briefly to meet my eyes. He stroked his thumb across his bottom lip and flashed me a fanged grin. "But it is hard to enjoy the company of such subpar women when we have such a goddess here at home."

I flushed at his flattery. "Stop it."

"It's true." Wynn moved away from the door and sauntered over to me like a panther on the prowl. He wore a pair of tight black jeans that hung low on his hips. His button-down shirt was the color of his eyes a royal blue that made his already intriguing eyes even more vibrant. His tattoo of the house sigil flashed beneath the shirt where he'd left it unbuttoned at his chest.

I held my hand not holding my towel up to stop him from coming any closer. My fingers brushed his cool chest which was in some ways even worse than having him close. My breath caught, and my eyes flicked from his face to his chest and back. I started to pull my hand away, but his long fingers grabbed mine to keep them there.

"You can touch me, Piper." The way Wynn said my name made my knees weak and my heart pound. It was like he was savoring a decadent chocolate cake and he couldn't wait for seconds.

As I licked my lips, I let my fingertips trail along the lines of his chest before pushing the side of his shirt away to reveal the house sigil. I traced the black letters of their house motto and then over the crow and branch. "Do all of you have this?"

Wynn's gaze softened. "Yes. We each got it the day we started our new house. It's a reminder of our bonds to each other and a reminder as well."

My eyes moved up to his. "A reminder of what?"

Wynn leaned down until our noses brushed and murmured, "Of where we came from and where we are determined never to go again."

I found myself tipping my head back. I didn't know if it was the lack of interaction the last few days or if it was Wynn using his powers on me. It could have been just the man himself, but whatever the cause was, I wanted Wynn to kiss me. I wanted it more than anything else in the world at that very moment.

I also knew that if Wynn denied me, I would be crushed. I'd been crushing on him since the moment I stepped foot in the Durand's household. While we'd teased and flirted, even had a small brush of the lips once, he had never kissed me the way I had dreamed of him kissing me. Not like Rayne had kissed me.

Oh, God. Rayne!

Remembering the redhead made me pull back from Wynn, no matter how much it pained me to do so. I forced my closed eyes to open and placed a finger on Wynn's lips to stop him from kissing me. His confused blue eyes met mine.

"I've kissed Rayne," I blurted out, my eyes wide. "I like Rayne. I mean... I like you too, but I don't know..." I dropped my hand and scratched the side of my head. "This is all so confusing. You guys are so... well, you know." I waved a hand at his hot body and then lost my words for a second, making Wynn chuckle. "Then you all come sniffing around with your pretty words and those bedroom eyes, and I lose my balance."

I huffed and crossed my arms over my chest. "I don't want to hurt any of you or cause a rift between you guys. You're brothers, and I'm just... I'm the maid."

Wynn stared at me for a moment, but then he nodded. "I understand, but there's something you have to understand as well, Piper." He paused and cupped both sides of my face. "We've been together for decades, some of us even longer. We are not unfamiliar with the concept of sharing."

As my heart beat rapidly in my chest at his words, Wynn leaned toward me. My eyes fluttered shut against my will, and I prepared for him to kiss me anyway, but his lips pressed against my forehead instead.

Then, before my eyes even fully open, he was gone.

CHAPTER 15
Allister

THERE'S NOTHING MORE AGGRAVATING than not having the perfectly ripe tomato. I know, I know. I'm a fucking vampire... but even though I didn't actually need to eat didn't mean I had to give up my love for cooking.

While Drake and I were alive, or human, that is, Drake would woo his ladies with his muscles and wit. I, on the other hand, used my cooking as my way into their hearts and their bedchambers.

Hence the tomatoes.

One cannot make a perfect garlic and basil pasta sauce with mushy tomatoes. Some might say they are going to be cut up anyway, but it's not just about texture. It changes the taste which meant the whole batch would have to be tossed and redone.

"Not the spaghetti, Al," Drake moaned as he came into the kitchen and glanced at my half-prepped meal. "You might as well kick us all out of the running for Piper if you are already pulling out your cooking."

"What can I say?" I smirked as he collapsed into one of the island chairs and leaned on his hand with a grumpy pout. "I play to my strengths."

Drake rolled his eyes. "You already have a strength. Use that silver tongue of yours to persuade your way into her panties, not your food." He gestured to the pan of simmering sauce. "It's just cruel."

I rolled my eyes. "And what will Piper do when she finds out I used my powers on her to seduce her?"

Drake shrugged as if he didn't care, but my brother wasn't the kind to put his emotions right out there, at least not to others. Being a twin did have its benefits. He cared far more than he let on, hiding his feelings behind his jokes and laughter. But I knew the real him. The real him loved poetry and was so romantic he threw his whole heart into every relationship, leaving me to pick up the pieces afterward.

"Do I smell Allister's famous spaghetti?" Rayne commented, sniffing the air as he strolled into the kitchen. He glanced inside the large pot of boiling noodles and then eyed me suspiciously. "What's the occasion?"

Before I could answer, my twin snarled, "He's cheating by winning over Piper's stomach first."

Rayne's head turned from Drake and then back to me. Arching a brow, he drawled, "Really? You realize she's a bottomless pit, right? She'll inhale this in two seconds without a thought. If you want to win her over, you're gonna need more." He picked up one of my left-over tomatoes and tossed it from one hand to the other with a grin. "Much more."

I grabbed the tomato midair and turned my back on them. "That's why this is just for her. Not any of you. So, hands..." I smacked Rayne's hand before he lifted the sauce spoon up to his mouth. "... off!"

Rayne stared hard at me as if tempted to reach for the spoon again before thinking better of it. He shrugged a shoulder and moved to the fridge instead. "Keep your noodles. You'll need them. I've already got a head start."

Drake threw his head back and laughed. "He has a point there, Al. Our little brother is already two steps ahead of us." He waggled his brows at Rayne.

"Don't call me that." Rayne scowled. "You know I hate that. I might have changed at a younger age than you, but we're damn near the same age now."

Drake lifted his hands and gave a lazy shrug. "What can I say? You look perpetually eighteen. I can't help but treat you like a kid."

Rayne gave him an incredulous glare before shaking his head and leaving. Drake and I exchanged a look and chuckled. He opened his mouth to say something else, but we both turned toward the back stairs and exhaled deeply.

Piper was coming.

While her bleeding period seemed to have ended, it didn't take away from the addicting scent of her everyday self that preceded her, a combination of lilacs and some kind of powder I could only assume came from her deodorant all enhanced by the very scent of her. It was a heady mixture, for sure.

"Do I smell spaghetti, Gretchen?" Piper grinned as she skipped down the steps. First, her lovely smooth legs came into view, and that was something I could stare at all day long, especially when she decided to wear a pair of those impractical shorts of hers. It was times like this that I wished the women in my human life hadn't been so prudish in their clothing choices. Not that any of them compared to the woman coming down the stairs.

No, Piper had an angelic like feel to her with just a touch of devilishness. She could give you the sweetest smile before snapping your head off for saying the wrong thing. I'd thankfully not been on the receiving end of one of those tantrums yet.

Her blonde hair framed her face like a halo, putting her rounded face and pert nose on display. Besides the mouth I couldn't stop dreaming about was the way she held herself, like she wasn't quite sure of her footing in the world. In a purely physical fashion, she had proven that by the many things her clumsiness has broken.

Another of Piper's many adorable quirks.

When her eyes landed on my brother and me, her steps faltered. She tripped over one step, and my brother and I were at her side in a flash, but it wasn't needed. She caught herself at the last moment.

"Uh..." She let out a shaky laugh as she wrapped her arms around her midsection, a motion that pulled up her t-shirt to show a sliver of skin. With her eyes bouncing between the two of us, she cautiously stepped into the kitchen. "You're not Gretchen."

Drake grinned. "Not since the last time I checked, but I'd be happy to let you do a full body search, if you like?" He held his arms out to the side and wagged his brows at her suggestively.

Piper blushed and ducked her head. "That won't be necessary."

That was my chance to get a word in. "Why don't you take a seat?" I gestured to one of the chairs at the island with my spoon. "It's almost done."

Her brows furrowed for a moment before she nodded. Piper slipped into the chair next to my brother, leaving the one on the other side of her open.

Perfect. It's like she was made for us. She automatically always tries to include all of us. I wasn't even sure she knew she was doing it.

Piper seemed at a loss for words. Her fingernails tapped on the island countertop as she rolled her bottom lip between her teeth. I stirred the pan of sauce with one hand while keeping an eye on her.

After a moment of us just staring at one another, she placed her hands on the counter and moved to get up. "I'm going to get a drink."

Drake was up and back in his seat with her usual beverage of choice, a can of coke, sitting in front of her before she even closed her mouth.

Mouth slightly agape, she blinked a few times before taking the can. As she cracked the lid open, Piper nodded toward Drake. "Thanks."

"My pleasure." Drake beamed, leaning on his hand to watch her.

I wanted to throw something at him. If my twin didn't stop staring at her like she was some kind of goddess, he was going to freak her out and ruin this for me. I couldn't have that.

"Drake," I stated with a stern tone, "don't you have that thing you need to attend to?"

Drake didn't even glance my way. "What thing?"

I resisted the urge to groan my frustration. "You know, the thing you were going to do that isn't in the kitchen?" I eyeballed him and let out an awkward chuckle as Piper surveyed us.

My twin finally stopped staring long enough to realize what I was trying to tell him. He dropped his arm and abruptly stood.

"Oh. Yeah. That thing. The thing that's in the..." He looked to me for guidance before finishing. "... garage. In the garage." He backed away from the island, gave Piper a small wave. then gestured to the back door with his thumb. "I'll just be in the garage. You know. Doing my thing. Uh. You enjoy your dinner. Al's a great cook," he added with a swing of his arms as he walked backward to the back door. "You're gonna love it."

"Thanks, Drake," I said with a shake of my head.

Piper glanced toward the door my twin just went out and then back to me before letting out a little giggle. "What was that all about?"

I lifted a shoulder and tried to play it off. "I'm his twin, not a mind reader. You'll have to ask Rayne about that."

My words made her clam up pretty fast, and I worried I'd said something wrong. However, before I had a chance to mention it, my timer went off. I turned back to the stove and twisted the knob for the burner before taking the sauce off it. I pushed a button on the oven and grabbed my oven mitt, pulling the garlic bread from the inside of the oven.

"Oh, God. You made garlic bread too!" I grinned over my shoulder to see her half-collapsed on the island with hungry eyes. "You're trying to fatten me up, aren't you?" She sat up abruptly and arched a brow. "This had all been some elaborate game to get me big and fat so you guys can eat me."

Dirty thoughts came to my mind immediately, and I had to turn my back so I could adjust myself. "Uh. Not in the way you mean."

Piper made a small sound of confusion before letting out a long oh. Her arousal spiked, the scent hitting my nose like a punch to the nuts which in turn made my current condition even worse. I cleared my throat and busied myself with getting the bread cut and the noodles and sauce combined. All the time, I prayed to whatever God there was that I didn't embarrass myself.

"So, where's everyone else?" Piper asked, finally killing the awkward silence.

I fixed her a plate as well as my own and prepared myself as I pivoted back around. "They're around." I placed Piper's plate in front of her before sitting down in the chair my brother had vacated. I didn't dig into my food right away. Instead, I waited to see Piper's reaction.

The little maid had no qualms about eating what was in front of her. Her mouth was already stuffed full the moment I sat the plate down. I couldn't help bit grin as she inhaled my spaghetti like she hadn't eaten in years.

After a moment, Piper realized she was being watched. She swallowed what was in her mouth and flushed with embarrassment as she turned to me. "Uh. It's really good."

I beamed at her. "Thanks."

Piper didn't seem to know if she should eat or not, so, to show her it was alright, I twirled a bit around my fork and stuck it in my mouth. Satisfied with my actions, Piper continued to eat but this time with a bit more care as if she were conscious of me watching her.

"So, you cook often?" Piper turned her head my way before taking a bite of her bread. Her eyes closed briefly, and I swore she let out a little moan that was doing nothing for my hard-on for her.

"I used to." I nodded and shifted in my seat. "Not so much since I became..." I trailed off, not knowing how exactly to describe why I stopped.

"A vampire," she finished for me with a small smile, not at all bothered by what I was.

"Yeah." I sighed. "A vampire. Food is still fun to eat, but we don't really need it to survive so it kind of puts a damper on the whole fun of it."

She nodded in understanding as she drank from her soda can. "I get it. Kind of like baking cookies when you're on a diet." I gave her a confused look. She waved her fork in the air as she tried to explain. "You know. Just the action and smell of it is enjoyable, but you know you don't really need it, but you put yourself through the motions of it anyway just because a part of you wants it." Piper gave me a shy smile before shoving a forkful of noodles into her mouth.

I couldn't stop smiling at her. She was just that amusing. "I wouldn't know. I've never been on a diet before."

With her mouth half full, Piper rolled her eyes and picked at her plate. "Of course not, you guys are chiseled out of granite. You need a diet like I need a..." She caught herself with a sheepish grin. "What I mean to say is, you look good."

"Thank you." I chuckled. "I'm pleased to know you feel that way."

She nodded absently, slowly chewing.

We sat there together in silence for a few moments. It wasn't an awkward one anymore, and neither one of us was in a rush to fill it. I only hoped one of my other brothers didn't ruin it by showing up for food. They didn't usually care for eating other things than blood, but if they knew Piper was here, they'd make some excuse. I was about to ask her if she wanted more but then she asked something else instead.

"You know, Wynn said something to me earlier or rather yesterday." Piper shifted in her seat, her fingers playing with her can of soda. "I was wondering if you could confirm what he said for me?"

My brows lifted. All manner of scenarios went through my head. It was Wynn after all. He could have said anything from bad-mouthing one of us to outing himself and, in part, the rest of us about the club. However, I didn't want to jump to conclusions or put ideas in her head, so I simply said, "Yes?"

Piper wouldn't meet my eyes, and a faint blush crossed her cheeks as she struggled to speak. "Well, I had concerns about letting him kiss me seeing as I'd already kissed Rayne." Her head dipped and her shoulders bunched up around her ears.

My lips ticked up at the sides already having an idea of where she was going with this, but I wanted to hear her say it. "Go on."

"Well," she cleared her throat and then met my gaze, "he implied, Wynn that is, that you guys have..." She stopped and slapped herself on the face with a distraught sound. "Sorry. Forget it. Forget everything I just said. It's stupid. I'm stupid."

Piper jumped out of her seat, but I was there before she could make her escape. She gasped and stepped back a step. I took that moment to capture her hand in mine and pull her back toward me.

"You want to know if we're okay with you kissing more than one of us? Is that what you're trying to ask?" I brushed a bit of her hair back from her face, enjoying the feel of her soft skin beneath my fingers.

Her mouth dropped open, and her breathing quickened. As she licked her lips, she bobbed her head. "Yeah. I mean, yes. He said you guys were into..." She seemed to struggle with her next word before she finally got it out. "... sharing."

I gave her a small smile as I tried not to laugh at her embarrassment. "Piper." Her brown eyes lit up as I said her name, her gaze meeting mine with a mixture of shyness and perhaps a hint of desire. "We've been with each other for a long time. Our definition of monogamy isn't the same as a human."

Her eyes widened substantially, and I quickly worked to explain further.

"Not to say that we wouldn't each be faithful to you, but we also have a fragile dynamic. Having more than one woman in the mix would complicate that even more than it already is with us all being crazy about you."

Piper let out a choked sound. "You... you are?"

I lowered my face close to hers and murmured, "Haven't you noticed, little maid? You have thoroughly captured the vampires of this house... or at least this one."

Her heart pounded rapidly in her chest, and her eyes fluttered closed as I moved in to finally capture those lips with mine... and I would have had the doorbell not just sounded through the house. The sudden sound jolted Piper, and she pushed me away with her small hands as she took a large step back.

With a shaky breath and a little laugh, she scrambled toward the kitchen door. "I better get that."

I scrubbed a hand over my face, cursing at her retreating figure when a hand clamped down on my shoulder. I knew it was my twin without having to look.

"Well, that's the breaks. My turn now."

CHAPTER 16
Piper

THE DOORBELL RINGING COULDN'T have come at a better time. If I hadn't known if I should kiss Wynn, I sure as hell shouldn't have been kissing Allister. Sweet, caring, such a fucking great cook Allister.

He had surprised me today. The quieter of the two twins, Allister hadn't said more than a few words to me since I started. Now, he was feeding me, a huge plus for him, and telling me I had the whole household wrapped around my finger? I could hardly believe it. Yet, he hadn't been acting like he was lying.

I chewed on that information on my way to the front door. Usually, Darren would answer the door, but he was in the office with Antoine 'helping' him with something. I have started to suspect his helping was more than in an employee-boss sort of way, especially considering the way the guys made not so subtle comments about the two of them.

A shudder of desire rushed through me and settled between my thighs at the thought. Either of them, Darren and Antoine, was any woman's wet dream, and the thought of them both together just did it for me. If I didn't know the house was full of vampires now, I'd sneak away to my room to play out what I hoped was going on up in Antoine's office. What I had instead were fantasies of what the commanding vampire might have done to me last time I was in there with Darren's help.

Wow, where'd that come from? Now, I was drooling after the only other human here. Jeez, Piper. You need to get laid and bad.

Shaking my head, I turned the doorknob and pulled it open. Plastering on my best customer service face, which was fake as all get out, I opened my mouth to greet whoever had come to call on my masters... except the words I had prepared to say died on my lips. Standing before me wasn't some visitor for the masters or even a delivery, that would have been sent to the kitchen, but my very own parents.

"Mom...? Dad...?" I gasped, my mouth hanging open as I took in my parents. Derek and Jennifer Billings were exactly what you would imagine a suburban couple would look like, wearing khaki pants and polo shirts along with sensible shoes and matching cardigans. They were everything I was not. Poised. Polite. Perfect. The three p's I was never able to achieve. That was one of the reasons we didn't exactly speak to each other anymore. What really broke the camel's back was when I refused to marry Brad, a boring cookie cutter that had the same ideals as my parents and their whole neighborhood of clones.

"Piper!" My mom scowled with a shake of her perfectly coiffed blonde hair. "Is that any way to greet your parents? And are you going to make us wait here on the doorstep all night or invite us in?"

Remembering myself, I swallowed and moved to the side. I started to let my parents in than I remembered an important detail about the household I lived in, vampires. My parents were humans. Nope. Nope. Nope. I couldn't let them in.

Jumping in front of them, I shook my head and tried to usher them back out. "Let's talk out here. You know the house is kind of a mess. I don't want you to see that."

"But aren't you the maid?" My dad cocked his head to the side with disapproval. "Isn't it your job to keep things from getting messy?"

I nodded slowly at a loss for words. "Uh, yes. That is my job. I clean the house, but you know, I was sick this week and haven't had a chance to catch up, and I'd hate to have you judge it based on that."

"Oh, nonsense." My mom shook her head and pushed her way in. I stumbled back and gaped at her, my eyes flicking to the door to the dining room and back to them. My dad followed close after her as each of them took in everything there was to see. I could tell by their expression that they approved wholeheartedly of the house I worked in. In fact, the way my mom was looking at me, I could see the wheels turning in her head.

Ugh. Why did they have to show an interest in me now? It has been five years, and now, now of all times to actually care what I was doing, they had to pick when I was working for vampires. Did someone up there have it in for me or what? I screamed silently up at the ceiling and simultaneously prayed the masters would keep their distance.

As if summoned by my very thoughts, Drake and Allister came through the dining room door. Their eyes were curious and confused at the sight before them, then they seemed to piece two and two together, and those confused looks turned to delight.

I was instantly suspicious.

I didn't want whatever they planned to get out of control, so I jumped in and gestured to the approaching twins. "Mom. Dad. These are two of the gentlemen I work for. Drake and Allister Durand." I gave them a warning look hidden beneath a fake smile. "Master Durandses," I winced as I struggled through the introduction, "these are my parents."

My mom practically melted on the floor and then hurried across the foyer to shake the twins' hands. "Oh, my. If my bosses were half as attractive as you two, then I might have stayed in the workforce after I got pregnant with little Peppy here."

Drake grinned at my mom and then, over her head, mouthed 'Peppy.'

I grimaced and repressed a groan. My mom was really trying to embarrass me here, and she'd just got in the door. My dad, however, wasn't looking at the twins like he was thinking of having an affair. Thank God, that would be weird.

Instead, he was giving them the stink eye, looking them over before asking with his not-at-all intimidating dad voice, "Master. huh? You have some kind of fetish about making my daughter call you that?"

The grin on Allister and Drake's faces dropped abruptly. This time, it was my turn to enjoy their discomfort. The twins fumbled for their words, making the two large men look flustered and adorable all at once. They were saved from coming up with an answer by Antoine as he appeared at the top of the steps with Darren in tow.

"My apologies if our ways seem a bit outdated," Antoine explained as he made his way down the left staircase. "In our country, it is common practice to refer to the employers by Master and Mistress."

His blonde hair was braided and draped over his shoulder, its paleness a stark difference to the midnight black dress shirt he wore beneath its matching suit jacket and pants. The only color in his outfit was the pure white tie with a pin in it decorated with a minute sigil of the house. If my mother had been near dead from the twins, she was about to have a heart attack at the sight of Antoine.

Jennifer Billings fanned herself as if she were having a hot flash, but I was pretty sure she was feeling exactly the same as I had been for the last few months. I covered my mouth with my hand and tried to hold back a laugh as my mom sort of danced across the foyer to stand before Antoine.

Darren arched an amused brow, meeting my gaze over the others from a few paces back on the stairs. He was as poised and put together as ever, not showing an ounce of what might have happened in the office upstairs. I returned his look with a shrug. I had no idea why they were here or that they were coming at all. The last I'd heard from them had been on my birthday when they gave me their obligatory card in the mail.

That had been six months ago.

My dad, however, was not impressed by any of this. He stepped in front of my mom and offered Antoine his hand with a flat expression. "Derek Billings, and where exactly is it you come from?"

Antoine took my dad's hand with his own and gave it a firm shake before answering. "All over. Mostly from Eastern Europe, but the twins have family in Brussels." He glanced back at Darren for a moment as if to confirm.

Darren nodded curtly. "Yes, Master Durand. Master Allister and Master Drake come from Brussels, Belgium."

My mom fluttered her lashes at the twins with a coy grin. "Well, you wouldn't know it, I can't hear an accent at all."

"We pride ourselves on being able to integrate into the American culture." Ever the flirt, Drake gave her a bashful grin. "We find it much easier to get along with others when we sound like we belong here. To hear you say that you couldn't tell is a great compliment from an even greater beauty."

As she giggled at Drake's words, my mom shot me a happy wink. "I like them. You should stay here."

I laced my fingers in front of me and pressed my lips together to repress a laugh as I met Antoine's eyes across from my dad. "I plan to. As long as they'll have me."

Antoine's brow lifted before he inclined his head in understanding, then he turned and quirked a finger at Darren.

"Please, have a room prepared for Miss Billings' parents and have dinner served in the dining room." He paused and watched my parents expectantly. "You are staying, aren't you? I wouldn't be able to forgive

196

myself for sending you home without at least a full belly."

"Of course, Master Durand." Darren gave a slight bow before giving me a meaningful look that I think meant he wanted to talk to me in private, but I promptly ignored it. No way was I leaving my parents alone with vampires.

"Mom, Dad." I placed a hand on my dad's shoulder. "Wouldn't you feel more comfortable at maybe a hotel? Or... oh!" I clapped my hands together once. "Aunt Doris. She lives in town. Maybe you could stay with her?"

"Miss Billings, I'm surprised at you," Antoine purred as he stepped into our little circle. "Why should your parents put up money for a hotel room when they can stay here? I'm sure they will want to spend as much time with their daughter as possible, and the added drive would take away from that."

As I gritted my teeth, I felt my eye twitch as I stared Antoine down, knowing that I couldn't outright say why I didn't want them to stay with them. Of course, Antoine didn't know that my parents and I didn't exactly see eye to eye, but I wasn't going to bring that up now either.

"But Master Durand," I bit out with a tight smile, "we are in the middle of preparations to leave tomorrow. I'm sure my parents don't want to be in the way."

Antoine placed his hands behind his back with a twinkle in his eyes. "Oh, it's no trouble at all. I'm sure you and Darren have it covered, but you do bring up a valid point." Antoine turned his gaze to my parents with an apologetic smile. "The whole household is going out of town tomorrow. So, we won't be able to host you but one night."

"Even Piper?" My mom glanced to me the first hint of worry on her face. Me working for hot guys in this big old house wasn't a problem, but God forbid I leave the state with them. Sometimes, I wondered if my mom had her priorities straight.

"Yes." Drake stepped in with a reassuring air. "Piper is pivotal to our trip. We are going to see the head of our... company." Those blue-green eyes met mine with a quirk of his lips before returning to charm my mom. "She not only takes care of the household but each of us individually as well. Usually, Darren only comes, but it's so much easier for us to have two for the six of us than one."

"Six?" My dad about choked on the word. "There are six of you?"

"Oh, yes." Drake beamed, clearly getting a kick out of messing with my dad. "Antoine is the oldest, and then there is Marcus, Allister and me, Wynn, and then the youngest Rayne."

"And you all live here?" My mom circled her finger in the air between us. "Together, in one house?"

I think my mom was just two seconds away from having an aneurysm right after my dad had a heart attack or worse, beat them within an inch of their lives. Or at least try to. Vampires versus my fifty-year-old dad? Now that would be a sight to see.

Ever the diplomat, Antoine nodded. "We are a very close-knit family. Private as well," he said as his eyes slid my way. "We like to keep things in the family as much as possible."

If the ground could swallow me up now, it wouldn't be soon enough. I swear the masters really wanted to drive me to an early grave. Forget meeting the sire or dealing with Valentine, they'd kill me with their teasing before my parents even left the house.

Darren, thank his beautiful head, appeared in the doorway of the dining room. "Please, this way. Dinner will be served shortly."

My mom and dad seemed to put aside their concerns for the moment with the announcement of food. They let themselves be led into the dining room with Antoine in the front and the twins behind them. I brought up the rear, trying to calculate the odds of them figuring out the masters' secret and if they would try to kill my parents if they did.

"Relax." Allister trailed back to clasp my hand in his. He gave it a squeeze as he leaned over to whisper in my ear. It wouldn't keep the others from hearing, but at least, my parents wouldn't. "We've played human for years. A few hours will be a piece of cake."

I rolled my eyes up to him. "Them finding out isn't the biggest concern I have right now."

"Oh?" Allister asked almost laughing at me. "Then what is?"

I stared straight ahead as I said, "That my dad will think you have less than honorable intentions toward his only daughter."

"Oh, but we do, little maid. We do." Drake barked a laugh as he winked over his shoulder and entered the dining room.

I let out a little whimper. "Can I just go back to hiding in my room? It has to be better than this?"

Allister took my arm in his and drew me toward the dining table. "Come now, the fun's just begun. The others haven't even arrived yet. And you know Wynn is just dying to meet your family."

"Oh, God. Kill me know." I leaned my forehead on his shoulder in agony earning me a chuckle from him and a strange look from my mom. I promptly moved away from Allister and moved toward the kitchen.

"Miss Billings?" Antoine's voice stopped me in the kitchen doorway. "Where are you going?"

My brows furrowed in confusion. "Uh, I'm going to help Darren in the kitchen?"

Antoine leaned back in his seat and urged me forward with two fingers. "Not tonight. Tonight, you have guests. You shouldn't work with your parents here. What kind of employee would I be if I made you do that?"

I eyed him for a moment thinking he might be pulling my chain and then when it seemed like he wasn't joking moved to the table. I took a seat next to my parents leaving an empty one on my right side between Antoine and myself. The twins took their seats across from my parents, then, as if being called by a dinner bell, probably some kind of vampire voodoo, the other three missing masters came walking through the dining room door.

There must have been some kind of memo about dressing up for dinner tonight because each of them was wearing their finest. Rayne had forgone his usual jeans and t-shirts to wear a pair of grey slacks and a white shirt accompanied by a slate blue tie. He seemed uncomfortable in the outfit but didn't fidget or complain. Marcus with his large frame and stoic personality went to his seat on Antoine's right side without a word, while Rayne gave me a curious look before taking the seat at the head of the table.

I met his eyes and tried to get him to read my thoughts. *Help. Save me. Get them out of here before they ruin everything!*

Of course, Rayne chose this moment to obey my wishes and keep out of my head. That or he flat out refused to help me. With the way he was so interested in my parents, I had to say it was the latter. To test my theory, I pictured myself pretending to drop my fork and climbing under the table. I crawled on the floor until I was right in front of where Rayne sat. As I dragged my hands up the inside of his thighs, I massaged him through his pants before pulling him from his pants and wrapping my mouth around his cock. I pulled him into my mouth as I moaned and sucked him hard until he cummed.

That made Rayne made a pained sound.

"You okay there, Master Rayne?" I smirked as I gave him a knowing look.

Rayne gave me a quick smile and cleared his throat. "I'm fine. Thank you for asking."

My mom was beside herself with all the new men coming in. I swear she was going to combust on the spot, soon to be followed by my dad who was looking more and more ill by the minute.

"Oh my, Piper, dear," Mom cooed. "You are so lucky to be surrounded by such fine attractive gentlemen every day. How do you get any work done?"

I gave her a tight smile. "I try my best."

Wynn was the last to enter. He didn't so much walk into the room but float. He'd actually thought to button up his blood red dress shirt this time, and I wasn't sure if it was already done that way or if it was for my parent's benefit. Either way, a part of me was sad not to be able to see his muscular planes of his chest. Just a small part but still...

"Well, what do we have here?" Wynn gave a sultry smile. "I didn't know you had a sister, Piper?" Wynn stopped at my mom's chair and picked up her hand to kiss it. The whole act made her giggle like a teenager.

I rolled my eyes and tried to gag at his corny lines. Antoine caught my eyes where he was leaning on one arm of his chair, his hand propped up at his face as those pale eyes watched me oh so carefully. I flushed and shifted in my seat but was unable to pull my eyes away from him.

Darren appeared which stopped Wynn from flirting even more with my mom. "It looks as if dinner has already been made so before I began to dish Allister's homemade pasta out, would anyone like a drink?"

I didn't hesitate to hold my hand up, ripping my gaze from Antoine's. "Me, please." I winced at how desperate I sounded, but when you were currently having dinner with your parents and not just one but six prospective males in your life who also happened to be vampires, alcohol had to be involved... or nobody was going to get through it alive.

CHAPTER 17
Rayne

DINNER WITH THE BILLINGS was an interesting affair indeed. Jennifer Billings had Piper's coloring but none of her spirit. It seemed she cared far too much about what others thought of her, and her mind was full of thoughts about which one of us she could get Piper to hook up with and possibly marry. I had to force back a grimace the couple of times she pictured Wynn or Antoine naked.

Ugh.

Derek Billings wasn't much better. The middle-aged man was more than a little bit suspicious of the six of us all living in one house together, not being married or having children with his darling daughter working alone with us every day. Apparently, Mr. Billings feared we'd take advantage of his innocent daughter.

I repressed a snort. It was we who were at her mercy, not the other way around. However, his worries weren't unwarranted. We all had our eyes set on the blonde maid, well, except Marcus, so I could understand his concern. Didn't make him any less annoying though.

"So, tell me, Antoine," Mr. Billings asked, his eyes hard as he stared at my older brother, "what exactly is it that you six do? You must be well off to own such a home and have servants. What is it?" He leaned forward on his elbow and bit out, his eyes narrowing as if he were going to get all of our secrets out of Antoine by just asking.

Pfft. I couldn't even find out what Antoine was thinking half the time, let alone get him to spill his guts. That guy was like an iron cage with the lock rammed so far up his ass, I'd be surprised if Darren could find it.

Antoine, always the one to take things with ease, lifted his glass of wine to his mouth. From here, I could smell the blood laced with it just like the rest of our glasses. He took a sip purely to make Mr. Billings wait for his answer. When Antoine finally lowered his glass, he leveled a look at Derek that made the old man flinch.

"We are involved with quite a few companies actually. We have our fingers in real estate as well as the healthcare industry and some nonprofits. And I'd hardly call our employees servants." His all-knowing eyes slid over to Piper, making her wiggle in her seat at the attention. "I like to think of us as a family. We have a bond that no other household could brag of, isn't that right, Piper?"

Piper flushed crimson, and my nose tickled with the scent of her arousal. She nodded slightly, unable to meet Antoine's gaze as her mind raced about something that had happened in the office the other day. I arched a brow at the head of our household, but he didn't acknowledge me. Antoine's eyes were all for Piper, something her father didn't care for one bit.

It was laughable really. While my brothers and I played human for Jennifer and Derek Billings, Piper seemed to be gritting her teeth and downing as much alcohol as possible. She laughed abnormally loudly and was overall trying to get through this dinner without her parents embarrassing her further or getting drained dry by us.

Like we'd lower ourselves that far. I rolled my eyes to myself.

However, Piper's relationship with her parents was now a mystery that I would have loved to unravel. She seemed to care about them a great deal, but they didn't exactly see eye-to-eye with her. Not that I didn't get that. My own parents weren't winning any awards, having left me to die the moment I showed the signs of my terminal illness. Some parents could handle such tragedies. Mine... just couldn't cope. So, I was left to sit in a hospital room all alone day in and day out as I waited for death to take me.

Antoine happened to be at the hospital for his monthly rations of blood that day when he found me. I was on a ventilator and had to be tube fed. On the last leg of my life, I knew I was going to die in the next few days. At least that was what I prayed, but Antoine, he saw me all alone without a flower or card or person to weep for me and stepped in. He touched my forehead and peered into my eyes as if staring into my soul.

I had thought he was some angel of death with his pale features and dark clothing, come to see if I was worthy of Heaven or Hell.

However, what he said to me as he stared down at my fragile, dying form stuck with me even now.

"You poor, poor boy. No one to love you. No one to care that you'll be gone. Do not worry, it will all be over soon."

Those words didn't comfort me. They scared me to death. I made a pained sound through the breathing mask, and tears slid down my face. I'd never told anyone about that day because it was when I was at my lowest, my absolute weakest. But, at that moment Antoine lifted me up. He saved me. Antoine and the others had been my family ever since.

Thinking back on those days and seeing Piper now, suffering to get through one meal with her parents, made me want to gather her up in my arms and tell her it was all going to be over soon, that we would be her family now.

As if feeling my eyes on her, Piper's gaze locked with mine. For a brief second, she didn't seem as miserable. She gave me a tiny smile and an eye roll. I gave her a discreet thumbs-up to show her that I was there for her which only made her smile more.

It was at that moment that I realized I didn't just want this human. I loved her. For the first time in my vampire life, I loved something more than blood, more than ever getting to see the sunrise again... and I had no idea how to tell her.

"Well," Derek Billings stood from the table and stretched his arms, "thank you for the meal, but I am beat. We drove quite a ways to check on my little girl." He placed a hand on Piper's shoulder and gave it a squeeze before looking to Antoine. "We'll take that room you offered us now, if you don't mind."

"Of course, forgive me. We have a lot of clients from the other side of the world, so our clock is a bit backward." Antoine inclined his head and gestured to Darren, but Piper stood abruptly.

"I'll take them. It's fine." She quickly waved Darren off and then gestured for her parents to follow her. "Come on, Mom, Dad. Let's leave them to finish their meal." As she passed by my chair, she gave me a sultry wink. I didn't need to read her mind to see what she was trying to tell me, but I did anyway.

Wait five minutes, then come to my room.

Let me tell you, those five minutes were the longest in my entire existence. It took everything I had to stay still in my chair and pretend like nothing had happened. I wasn't sure what she wanted for sure, but I was hopeful. Hopeful enough to be rock hard in my seat. I shifted uncomfortably.

"So, what did you think?" Drake asked, holding his cup with both hands. "About Piper's parents?"

Wynn snorted and rolled his head toward Drake with a lazy grin. "They're pretentious wannabes. I have no idea where our precious Piper came from, but it definitely wasn't them."

"Right?" Drake sat forward in his chair, disbelief growing on his face. "They're so different. I mean, our parents," he gestured to Allister and himself, "weren't the greatest either, but man, these two really take the cake."

I bobbed my head in agreement, pretending to pay attention to their conversation but too anxious about going to meet Piper to really listen.

"It is no surprise that Miss Billings came to work for us," Antoine announced as he held his glass up for Darren to refill. "They are not the kind of people she would ever become."

"You've got that right." Allister scoffed and made a face. "They seem like the type to live in one of those neighborhoods with rules about how high your grass could be. Piper forgets to put the milk back... a lot."

We all nodded. Piper and her parents were apples and oranges. It was clear why she didn't have much of a relationship with them. However, it made me wonder what they were even doing here now.

"I think they are up to something," I said out of the blue. That got everyone's attention.

"Did you hear something?" Drake asked with a tense clench of his jaw. How easily he became enraged when it came to our maid. It was a wonder she hadn't been taken fully by any of us yet.

"No." I shook my head sadly. "Her father mainly kept making snarky remarks about us being deadbeats who wanted to defile his precious daughter." The twins and Wynn chuckled at that, and even Antoine smirked. "And the mom..." I shuddered as I laced my fingers in front of me. "... wouldn't stop picturing you all naked."

Most of the others shared my sentiment with a shudder and a few gagging noises. Antoine didn't react much at all though, and Marcus just looked bored.

Tapping a finger against the side of his face, Antoine leveled a look at me. "What makes you think they are not being truthful?"

I shrugged a shoulder. "They obviously don't have a great relationship. Piper doesn't seem very happy to see them here. In my experience, that means they want something." I shifted in my seat. I should have kept my mouth shut because now, they were going to want to discuss it, and Piper was waiting for me.

"If they aren't here to check up on her, what do you think they want?" Wynn mused as he laid his head on the table as he played with his wine glass.

"Probably money." Drake snorted, and his twin nodded in agreement. "Most family members will only put aside their differences for a few things, and money is at the top of them."

"Well, we can only hope that is the reason." Antoine stood from the table and adjusted his suit jacket. "We have it in abundance and can easily get rid of them. We don't need any further complications. Marcus?"

He didn't wait for the large stoic vampire to answer before leaving the dining room, but Marcus followed our eldest without a word. Meanwhile, Darren disappeared into the kitchen as the other kept trying to guess what Piper's parents wanted. Thankfully, since half of the party had left, I could make a quick exit which I did with the excuse of going to my room.

Once I arrived at the top of the stairs, I didn't turn right to go to my bedroom but instead turned left towards Piper's. Her parents were in the room at the end of the hall, closest to the back stairs which meant Piper's was far enough away for them not to hear us.

I approached her door and lifted my hand to knock, but at the last second, I decided not to and tried the handle instead. When it turned, I peered around the hallway to be sure no one saw me before slipping inside.

Piper wasn't in her room, but the sound of water running in the sink came from the bathroom. I closed the door softly and moved to take a seat to wait for her. Before I could make it two steps, her voice rang out in my head.

Lock the door.

I did as Piper commanded without question, but the locked door and prospect of what might happen had my already hard cock pressing against the zipper of my pants. Not trusting myself to sit down, I walked over to her dresser and picked up a bottle of perfume.

Sniffing it, I groaned.

Fucking hell. As if I wasn't horny enough.

"Do you like it?" Piper asked, and I turned toward her voice.

"What?"

She stood in the bathroom doorway in a pair of those tiny pajama shorts and a thin tank top. I could see the outline of her nipples through it, and I almost dropped the bottle in my hand.

Piper nodded toward the bottle. "The perfume. I just bought it last week."

I glanced to the bottle and then back to her before nodding dumbly. "Uh, yeah. It's nice." I moved to put it back, but she had somehow gotten across the room without me realizing it.

Taking the bottle from my hands, she spritzed some on her wrist. "Here, it smells better on." She offered me her wrist, and two parts of me ached with wanting. My fangs wanted nothing more than to sink into her flesh and taste her and the perfume while my cock needed to be inside of her as well.

As I tried to hold back both parts of me, I leaned forward slightly and took a small sniff. The vanilla and lilac scent mixed with her own was a heady combination that made me want to rub myself all over it. Not trusting myself to behave, I stepped away from her wrist and glanced around her room.

"So, what did you want to talk about?"

"Don't you like it?" Piper peered up at me with those big brown eyes, and I couldn't look away. "Here, try it on my neck. It's even better." She sprayed some of the perfume herself and arched her head to the side, offering me the pulsating vein she had just made even more entrancing.

If I thought I was having a hard time holding back before, I was about to burst right there in my pants, and that was all because of a little perfume. That was until I heard her thoughts.

What is he just standing there for? I'm practically naked, offering him my neck. Is he just dense, or am I not that attractive?

"No!" I grabbed her arm with wide eyes. "I mean, no. It's not that. You're very attractive." Her brows furrowed, then her mouth fell open as she realized I'd read her thoughts again. "And it's not that I don't want to... but you've been drinking, and your parents are here, so that's probably got your head all kinds of messed up. I don't want to be that guy."

"What guy?"

I sighed and dragged a hand through my hair. "You know, the one you sleep with to get back at your parents and regret it in the morning."

Instead of freaking out like I thought she would, Piper smiled at me. She took a step

216

closer and grabbed the front of my shirt. "You think that's what this is?"

"Isn't it?" I frowned my own heart beating a mile a minute as I hoped against hope that I was wrong.

Piper shook her head, and her blonde hair swayed with the movement. "No, I like you, Rayne. Yeah, you can be kind of a jerk, but we have something here." She pressed her chest against mine, and I groaned at the feel of her nipples rubbing against me. "And as far as drinking goes, I had two glasses. I'm hardly drunk. I can still rock your world and not have a hangover in the morning."

I smirked and placed my hands on her hips. "You think so, huh?"

She grinned and nodded. "I know so." Piper trailed her hands up my chest and wrapped them around my neck, playing with the hair at the nape of my neck.

I was having a hard time finding any other excuse, so I allowed myself to enjoy the feel of her. My hands moved from her hips to her backside, and I used that new grip to pull her closer until our noses touched. "And your parents?"

Piper ground her hips against my erection making me groan in need. "What parents? I only see two people here, and that's you and me." She pointed a finger to each of us before pressing her lips against mine.

That was it. I could only take so much before I gave in. Piper had reassured me on both reasons I had to not do this, and she clearly still wanted to. Though a small part of me wondered why now of all nights, that part was overcome by the need to be inside of her.

I nipped at her lips, and Piper opened up to me, allowing my tongue to tangle with hers. I used my hands on her butt to lift her, and she promptly wrapped her legs around my waist with a moan. Our mouths still molded together, I walked us over to her bed and slowly lowered her onto it.

As I hovered over her, I ground my cock into the thin material covering her center. I could feel her heat coming through, and I could hardly take it much longer. I lifted one hand from her butt and cupped her breast, pinching her nipple through the material as I ravished her mouth. Piper bucked against me to rub her dripping center against the front of my pants. They were probably getting ruined, but I didn't care. I'd ruin all of my clothing to be doused in the scent of Piper aroused and wanting me like this.

Piper pulled back from my kiss and gasped for breath. She turned her head to the side, allowing me to trail my mouth down her throat as her hands made quick work of my shirt. I teased her with my fangs, my muscles tensed as her fingers played with my abs, lingering on the line of my pants. I pushed my hips toward her to urge her to take me in her hands.

Do you have a condom?

I lifted my head from her neck and arched a brow. "I'm a vampire. We don't have any diseases."

Piper's face was beat red as she asked, "And what about... babies?"

"Have you ever seen a vampire baby?" I asked, not quite believing we were having this conversation.

Piper's brows furrowed as she pulled back from me. "Why would I have ever seen one? I'd never seen a vampire until you guys. So, excuse me for not knowing how all this works. I just don't want to be knocked up by a vampire who is also kind of my boss."

"Don't say that." I tried to dissuade this line of thought quickly. We were getting off topic, and what we were progressing to would quickly end before it even began if we didn't get back to it.

"No, no. I will say it." Piper pushed at my chest, and I rolled off her with a dejected sigh. "I'm the help. I can't sleep with you."

She gasped and stood, her hands grabbing at her hair. "Oh, my god. I can't have sex with any of you. I'd be a prostitute."

"Really?" I lifted my brows and stared at her. "We're not paying you to sleep with us or even feed us. Just to clean our house, and, let's be frank, you don't even do that very well." I knew I had said the wrong thing the moment it came out of my mouth, so I sat up and held my hands open, trying to apologize. "Look, Piper, I didn't mean—"

"Get out." She glowered at me, crossing her arms over her chest. "You're right, this is a mistake. I want you to leave."

I stood and moved toward her, but she backed away. "Piper. Come on. I... I didn't mean that. Sometimes my mouth gets away from me."

Piper locked eyes with me and spat out, "Well, obviously you did, or you wouldn't have said it. Just go."

I reached for her a third time but then dropped my hand, not wanting to make her even madder. With my cock painfully erect, I didn't bother buttoning my shirt back up as I walked to the door. After I opened it, I paused and looked back at her. "I really am sorry, Piper."

She glanced over her shoulder and said, "Me too."

CHAPTER 18
Piper

I DIDN'T KNOW WHAT I had been thinking. No, I knew what I'd been thinking. I'd been feeling like crap because my parents had shown up. Add alcohol to the mix, and I just needed someone to make me feel better.

Sure, Rayne and I had been playing this back and forth act for a bit now, and I probably shouldn't have tried to make our first time something to boost my confidence, but then again, I should have known he'd ruin it somehow. He always did. You know, for a mind reader, he really didn't think before he spoke.

After Rayne left, I was irritated and still horny as fuck. I didn't give a crap if any of them heard me, so I climbed into my bed and finished what I thought was going to happen with Rayne. When I came, it was hollow and unsatisfying. I wanted to hunt him down and apologize for freaking out, but I was too much of a coward to do that. Besides, I had my parents to worry about, I couldn't be thinking about the masters right now.

But tell that to my mind which gave me endless dreams of the masters all night long that left me tossing and so turned on that I had to take a cold shower the moment I woke up. That alone should have told me how the rest of the day was going to go. Instead, I pulled on a pair of jeans and a yellow V-neck shirt and headed to my parents' room.

As I got closer though, I realized they weren't even in their room. I could hear my mom's over the top laughter coming from the bottom of the back stairs. Why were they already up this early? I mean, I was used to being up before seven, but my parents had never been the type to roll out of bed before nine, not unless my dad had a sunrise tee off.

What kind of game were they playing?

I wasn't stupid. I knew my parents. They didn't just drop in unannounced to see how I was doing. The last time I had spoken to them, they hadn't given two shits about me and were more worried about getting to some dinner party they were going to. Now, for them to show up out of the blue and pretend to be all charming and protective over me was suspicious, that's what it was.

They wanted something, and I was going to get to the bottom of it while avoiding Rayne at the same time.

After making my way down the back stairs to the kitchen, I prepared myself for all manner of scenes. My parents could be real dicks when they wanted to be, but they could also make anyone love them, even a stupid, gullible daughter who should know better.

"Oh, Piper, darling." My mom cooed from the kitchen table in the corner. "Come and have breakfast with us. Darren here was just regaling us with the tale of how you came into the Durand's' employment."

I shot an annoyed look in Darren's direction, but the butler just arched a brow and continued to pour my dad a cup of coffee at the island where he sat. Seeing that I wasn't going to get out of it, I pretended not to be bothered by my humiliating first-day story as I went to get coffee.

After grabbing a cup from the cupboard, I waited for Darren to bring back to the pot to whisper to him harshly, "Don't tell them anything. They're the devil."

Darren gave me an amused smirk before pouring coffee into my cup. While I filled my coffee with enough sugar to turn a weaker person into a diabetic, my mom continued to talk.

"Piper, dear, you know you are awfully clumsy and should have been more careful. You're lucky they didn't sue you for that vase." She sipped primly from her coffee cup while smiling at me over the rim. "It's just like that one time with the antique tea set you got for your birthday." She turned her eyes to Darren with a gleeful tone. "She hadn't had it longer than it took to unwrap it before it was in a million pieces on the floor. Poor Nana was devastated."

My mom pouted like it was the end of the world, But I wasn't fooled.

"Well, that will teach you to give a five-year-old a glass tea set for their birthday." I tried my best to keep the venom out of my voice, but it was hard when I had a lifetime of crap like that coming from the people who were supposed to love me the most in this world.

"Piper, don't sass your mother." My dad looked up from the newspaper to reprimand me. "She cared a lot about that tea set."

I sneered. "Yes, more than your five-year-old daughter who ended up with ten stitches to go with her birthday cake."

Darren's jaw ticked next to me, but he didn't say anything. I knew I was airing our dirty laundry in front of him, but my mom had started it.

"Piper Marie Billings!" my mom gasped. "You'll make poor Darren here get the wrong idea about us. I was simply stating a fact about your mannerisms, and here you are, putting me on the chopping block as a bad mother."

I almost choked on my coffee. "Bad mother? Ha. You only care about yourself and what the neighbors think."

"That's not true," my mom simpered, then took a drink from her cup as she pretended to compose herself. "I care about you a great deal."

I snorted and opened my mouth to retort, but it was Darren who swooped in.

"And when Piper was living in her car," Darren asked with a hint of animosity, "where were you then?"

My parents were befuddled by Darren's words as I gaped at him. My dad was the first

225

one to react, and that reaction was to slam his cup down on the island, the contents sloshing over the side of his cup.

"Piper got herself into that position, not us," he growled. "I do not like what you are insinuating."

Darren gave him a cool stare. "I'm not insinuating anything. I'm stating a fact. You claim to care about your daughter, but you would let her live in her vehicle? I have a hard time believing that."

My mom finally got herself together enough to snipe back. "Oh, we offered to let her live with us, but then again, Piper always does like to leave out the truth." She narrowed her eyes at me with a cold glare.

"Live with you?" I let out a hard laugh. "Don't even try that. You wanted me to come back and pretend to be your perfect daughter, marry Brad, and have babies you could brag about to all the neighbors." I took two steps toward the island, clacking my cup down on the top but, unlike my dad, not spilling a drop. "You only care about me when I can do something for you. You can see why living in my car was a better alternative."

"Oh, so dramatic you are," my mom groaned and rubbed the side of her head as if she were getting a migraine. "Can you blame me for wanting grandchildren? For wanting to see you taken care of?"

"I don't need to be taken care of," I hissed without a care about whether I was being loud or not. Let the whole house hear them, then maybe Antoine would throw her parents out on their asses like they belonged. "I certainly don't need taken care of by that snobby, 'have you seen my boat,' date rapist Brad Mulberry!"

My mom gasped, and my dad cried out, but I was already done with the conversation. I shook my head, snatching up my mug before I turned to the sink. I dumped my precious coffee out and offered Darren an apologetic smile before stomping out of the room.

I marched through the dining room and into the foyer where I flopped down on the bottom two stairs. It wasn't the best hiding place, but I could always make a run for it if I needed to. Thankfully, my parents didn't come after me. Probably too busy griping about what an ungrateful brat I was and making excuses to Darren.

I huffed a laugh. "So, stupid," I muttered to myself. Why should I have believed this time would be any different than before? They didn't care about me, only how I could make them look better, even if that meant sucking it up and marrying an asshole like Brad. I'd rather marry all six of the vampires here than that. At least then I'd get to live forever.

"Would you like me to get rid of them?"

My head jerked up from where I'd been fighting back my tears to see Marcus walking down the stairs behind me. It was surprising to see him, let alone hear him talk. I'd been getting the feeling that he didn't like me very much.

"I don't know. Yes. No." I gave him a helpless shrug and shook my head. "They'll just keep coming back until they tell me what they want, as always."

"Some parents should not have been," Marcus stated when he stopped at the bottom of the stairs to look at down at me.

I glanced up at him with a watery grin and laughed. "I feel that. Sometimes I wish I'd been born to different parents. Better ones. Ones that wouldn't try to make me into something I'm not."

"No." His sharp words made me frown. "Different parents mean a different you, and you are is quite remarkable."

I was speechless. Marcus was right, of course. If I had been born into a different family, there was no telling if I would have turned out differently. I could have been just as bad as Brad, full of myself and thinking the world owed me something. Still, it was funny to hear a compliment of any kind coming from the stoic vampire before me.

I angled my head back to meet his gaze. "Thanks, I think." I giggled nervously and wet my lips. "I thought you didn't like me? That I was a complication?" I mimicked his deep voice with a lopsided grin.

Marcus crossed those large biceps over his chest and peered down at me. "You are, but no one should be treated that way by their family."

"You're right." I nodded briskly. "They shouldn't. Family doesn't treat each other like that."

"Good, then they are no longer your family," Marcus replied curtly. I stared up at him in confusion. "Now, you are our family. We can throw them out."

He turned on his heels and started for the kitchen. I jumped to my feet and darted in front of him. With my hands up in front of me, I stopped him from moving forward.

"Hold on a second, big guy. As much as I would love to get rid of them, they're still my parents." I sighed and gave a small shrug. "I still love them."

Marcus watched me for a long minute before giving me a small nod. "Very well. Hear them out, then get rid of them."

I chuckled. "Sounds like a plan."

Marcus moved to leave, but I stopped him with a hand on his arm. He was so warm, like a big teddy bear. Shaking the inappropriate thoughts from my head, I grinned shyly up at him.

"Thanks, Marcus. Again. I really appreciate it."

"You're welcome." He inclined his head and then paused before adding. "Don't fuck my brothers over."

I gaped before barking a laugh so hard that I had to clutch my stomach in pain. I gasped and snorted as I giggled, falling against the wall as I tried to catch my breath. I heard a rush of footsteps, and then Darren asked, "What's wrong?"

Still laughing my ass off, I barely made out Marcus's reply. "I broke her."

That only made me laugh even harder. Now, I really had tears in my eyes as they poured down my cheeks. I let myself slide down the wall and sit on the cold floor, not caring that the two men were staring at me like I'd grown a second head.

What finally killed my laughing spree was my mom kneeling in front of me to cup my face in her hands. "Piper, are you alright? Stop laughing. It's not becoming. You sound like a braying donkey."

I shook my head and pushed her hands away. After catching my breath, I asked through a chuckle, "What do you want, Mom?"

My mom's brows furrowed. "What do you mean?"

"I mean," I grunted as I stood back up, "why are you here? You had to have come all this way for a reason. So... out with it." I waved a hand at her to prompt her to tell me what she came to say.

Mom bristled for a moment, and I could see the lie formulating in her eyes. Then she remembered Darren and Marcus's presences. "I believe that is a private matter."

I scoffed and rolled my eyes. "Of course, it is." I pushed past her and walked toward the foyer. "Come on, let's get this over with."

She went and got my dad before hurrying after me and into the foyer. Darren stopped me before I closed the sliding doors.

"You know that won't keep them from hearing you right?"

"I'm counting on it," I said with a wink before closing the doors to face my parents head-on.

CHAPTER 19
Piper

THE MOMENT I SHUT the doors, I breathed deeply. I had a feeling this was going to be another shooting match, but I was determined not to be the one to start it.

Like Marcus said, I had a family now. I'd only been with the Durands for a short while, but already, I feel more at home with them than I ever had with my birth family. Though with the parents I had, it wasn't hard to see how anything else was preferable.

I inched around to face my parents who had taken up residence on one of the chairs. It was like they are posing for a portrait or something. My dad sat in the chair with one arm wrapped around my mom's waist while she sat on the arm. Her legs were crossed neatly at the ankle as she leaned into my dad. The look on their faces already had my butt clenching in preparation.

"Piper," my dad started with a weary sigh, "we're worried about you."

I opened my mouth to say something snarky, but my mom held up her hand.

"Now before you get defensive like you do, just hear us out." She gestured for me to sit across from them, but I refused. Sometimes I was childish, but who doesn't revert when their parents are involved?

When my parents saw that I wasn't about to give them an inch, my mom and dad exchanged a look, the kind that most couples who have been together for a while did where they almost had a telepathic conversation. I resisted the urge to snort. If only they knew what a real telepath could do.

Thinking of Rayne made my stomach flutter. I didn't know what I was going to say to him next time I saw him... and that might very well be soon. We'd almost had sex, for crying out loud! How did you look your employer in the face after that?

"Piper? Are you even listening?" My mom's shrill voice interrupted my thoughts.

I shook the thoughts of the sexy redhead away and focused on my parents. "No, not really."

My mom huffed, and my dad patted her on the hip as if to calm her down. "Why are you even bothering to hear us out if you aren't going to listen to a word I say?" she cried.

I cringed at the high-pitched sound of Mom's voice and tried to look contrite, but I was sure I probably just looked constipated. I wondered if the masters had come inching up from the basement to hear what was going on yet? Marcus was probably still out there with Darren, but I doubted either of them would go and get the rest. I was hoping for some back-up with my parents without having to ask for it.

"As your mother and I were trying to tell you," my dad continued as if I had actually been listening or caring what they were talking about, "we want you to move in with us."

"No way," I snapped and glared at the two of them. "I already told you that before. I'd rather live in my car again."

My mom lifted her eyes to the heavens. "Please not that again. That was so embarrassing. How do you think it feels to tell your friends and family that your daughter lives in her car?" She shuddered and looked like she was going to be sick.

"Of course, it's all about how you feel, not how I felt, the person who actually had to live like that." I scoffed and turned away from them. "Just say what you need to say and leave."

"Now, don't be so hasty Piper." My dad's lips were pressed into a hard line much like his expression. "We have amended our offer."

"What? Now I can stay with you as long as I let some old lech rail me, so you get grandkids and he dies before I become an old maid to leave me his great estate?" I let my voice fill with how disgusted I felt about the whole thing. I wasn't some prized mare to auction off to the highest bidder.

"No, of course not. Don't be ridiculous." My mom scoffed, placing a hand on her chest as if she were appalled by the whole thing. "We want you to come work for your father."

I stared at them for a moment, stunned into silence. My dad wasn't the richest man, but he did well for himself with the accounting business. I had no skill with numbers so the thought of even trying to calculate anyone's books made me nauseous.

"Doing what exactly?" I drew out with an arched brow. "Taxes? Crunching numbers?" I shuddered and recoiled into myself. "Talking to clients?"

"Oh, God, no. Piper, you don't have the qualifications for any of that." My dad shook his head with a frown. "You would man the phones. What you were doing before...." He trailed off as he waved a hand around us. "All this."

"Yes." My mom nodded eagerly. "You'll have a real job again, not some menial servant labor." She made a face and lifted her nose in the air.

My mom has never washed a dish or cleaned a toilet in her life, so it wasn't a surprise that she found my current job demeaning... but I didn't. I liked my job. Sure, I wasn't the best at it, but I would get better in time. I knew exactly what I needed to do every day and I got to be active, something I never got at my desk job. And let's not forget that my bosses were hotter than hell. There's no way I'd trade this for some desk job with my dad. I might as well become an old maid now.

"Thanks, but no thanks," I told them with a satisfied smile. I dusted my hands off and stood. "Now, if that's everything. I have to prepare for our trip."

"But you haven't even heard the best part." My mom stood and walked over to me, grabbing my arm before I could leave.

I paused because she was my mom. If she had been anyone else, I'd have told her to get her hands off of me and go to hell.

"What's the best part?" I asked with a sigh. My eyes darted to the closed sitting room door, praying Rayne would hear me and come bursting in here so I'd have an excuse to leave. I didn't care if things would be weird between us now, I just wanted out of here.

My mom tightened her fingers on my arm, making me wince until I paid attention to her. "The best part," she began gleefully as if it were something that she was happy to tell me about, "is that Brad's older brother John has joined your father's firm. So, you'll be working closely with him every single day."

I didn't have a chance tell them how horrifying that actually was to me, John was even worse than his brother, because the sitting room door burst open, and not one Durand but all six of them came barreling into the sitting room. Antoine lead the group, his hair mussed like he'd just woken up but he was somehow already in a suit.

"I apologize for the intrusion, but since you are trying to poach my employee in my household, I feel that it is justified." He gave them a professional smile that was sharp enough to peel the skin off a potato.

"Excuse us, this is a family matter." My dad stood and marched over to Antoine, standing toe to toe with the vampire.

"You're right, it is," Drake stepped next to Antoine with Allister flanking Antoine's other side, "and Piper is part of this family. So, anything you have to say to her..."

"... you can say to us." Allister finished with his arms crossed over his chest, his muscular form towering over my dad.

My dad, to his credit, didn't so much as flinch. His nostrils flared as he glared at the men filling the room. "I won't have my daughter be sullied by the likes of you, no matter how much money you have."

"Oh, but I thought that was all that mattered to you?" Rayne stepped out from behind the group of vampires, his brows arched. "Or didn't you say your practice was going under, and that if you didn't get Piper to marry that ass wipe John, then you would lose everything?"

I wanted to be surprised, I really did, but it was just another in a long line of sins my parents had done against me. I sighed, suddenly tired of this whole thing and really wanting to go back to bed.

"Piper, dear!" My mom reached for me, but I shook her arm away. "You wouldn't want your parents to be homeless, now would you? Don't you love us?"

I let out a bitter laugh and shook my head before moving over to the Durands. "I honestly don't know anymore. I've made excuses for you over and over again, and every time, you're a disappointment. This is just too far." I stopped by Antoine and met his eyes, the steel in them softening slightly for me. "I might be doing a job you don't approve of, but these men have done nothing but make me feel important and needed. I'm not just something to show off to their friends or make a dime off of. And even though I've cost them quite a lot in the things I've broken, I'd like to think my friendship and presence here more than makes up for it."

Drake snorted. "Almost."

I shot him a 'oh, really' look. Antoine's hand slipped into mine, a shock to be sure, but I held on to it. He gave that hand a squeeze of encouragement.

With him next to me and the rest of them at my back, I turned to my parents and said, "I will not be leaving with you. If that means you lose your home and have to live on the streets, then... you did it to yourself." I parroted back my dad's words at him with a bit of satisfaction.

My mom gaped at me and then looked between my dad and me. Her lower lip quivered a moment before the tears started. She collapsed on the ground and wailed at the top of her lungs.

The Durands tensed around me, and I didn't blame them. I was no stranger to my mom's fits, except this time, I wasn't going to bend over backwards to make her happy. I was going to make me happy, and the Durands made me happy.

"Look what you did now," my dad hissed, his eyes burning holes into me. "You've broken your mother's heart. Are you happy with yourself? Do you feel good?"

I looked away from him and to the men around me before nodding. "Yes, I do."

"Time to go." Marcus came up to my dad, his big muscles flexing and those dark eyes hard and dangerous.

My dad stared up at Marcus with a slack jaw, then shook his head as his face contorted in anger. He opened his mouth to no doubt yell some more, but Antoine stepped in.

"Enough." That one word reverberated through the sitting room, and my dad and even my mom quieted. "You will leave this house, and unless she comes to you first, never bother Piper again. Do you understand?"

My mom and dad nodded dumbly.

"Darren?" Antoine turned his head to the side toward the butler. "Please gather the Billings belongings, and escort them off the premises."

"As you wish, Master Durand." Darren gave a slight bow before leaving to do exactly as Antoine said.

Antoine still kept a hold of my hand as he ushered me out of the sitting room and into the foyer. When we stopped at the bottom of the stairs, he turned me to face him. His hand came up to stroke the side of my face before dropping to his side, leaving a trail of hot fire behind.

"Why don't you go get packed?" he asked softly. "We're leaving in an hour." He then spun on his heel and walked away, leaving me to stare after him.

"That's it?" I asked as I turned back to the others back at the others.

They just chuckled and shrugged.

CHAPTER 20
Drake

SEEING DARREN ESCORT PIPER'S parents out was a surreal moment. My and Allister's parents weren't overly attentive. They were rich aristocrats, so as long as we promised to marry the women they chose for us and didn't create any bastard children, we could do whatever we wanted.

To see Piper's parents treat her like she was just some cash cow made me furious, so much so that I had to excuse myself back downstairs to cool off. I paced the floor of the basement with angry strides and dragged my hand through my short hair every half a dozen steps or so.

The others were busy getting ready to leave, but Allister sat there on his bed and watched me with concern.

"Stop it already, you're making me dizzy," he said with a sigh. "I know you're pissed. We all are. We heard what they were saying to her."

I paused in my pacing to stare at my brother, my breathing hard and my nostrils flaring. "It's just so demeaning. So inhumane. I mean, we're vampires for fuck's sake, and even we thought they were out of line." I let out a rough laugh. "I mean, who does that? And to their own child?" I rubbed a hand over my face and shook my head for what had to be the hundredth time.

"The same people who raised you," Wynn commented from where he lounged on his bed.

I spun around to face him and glared. "What did you say? Do you want to get knocked out?"

"Do you really think your parents were that different?" Wynn's head lulled from one side to the other as he arched a brow at me. "Think about it, they wanted you to marry who they wanted, and that meant whoever

243

benefited them. Financially, socially, and so on. It's not much different than what Piper's parents were trying to do to her except they were far more devious about it and..."

"Total dicks," Rayne inputted with a snarl. He acted like he wanted to rip their heads off their shoulders rather than sending them on their way after being worked over by Antoine.

I was right there with him.

"I can't believe we just let them go," I huffed and punched my fist into my open palm. "We should have eaten them for dinner."

Wynn scoffed. "And how do you think that would have gone over with Piper? Oh, yes, Piper, we have a lovely vintage from your parents. Now, please, open those delicious legs of yours and let me stick my cock in you." The prat sat up and fluffed his open neck shirt as he rolled his eyes at me. "Yes, I can see that going over really well, can't you?"

"Fine," I snapped as I stomped toward him, "then we should have snapped their necks. That'd solve all of their and our problems."

Marcus made a disgusted sound. "Such barbarians."

I spun on my heels and pointed a finger at the brute. "Like you have any room to talk. You're Antoine's enforcer. You wanted to get rid of Piper from the beginning. You have no room to judge me."

"Get rid of?" Marcus shook his head. "No, fire. Yes, she's... distracting."

The others hummed in agreement. Even I couldn't argue with that.

"Yeah, a tempting distraction, but one that we've already claimed as our own. We might as well make it permanent, you know?" I tried to urge my brothers to the same conclusion I had come to. Binding her to us was all good and well, but those bonds could be undone if one tried hard enough. It might deter Valentine, but it wouldn't stop him, not forever.

"You're wanting to make her one of us?" Rayne gaped at me, irritatingly having read my mind. "Are you crazy? She'd never go for that."

"How do you know?" I gestured at him aggressively. "Have you asked her? She might find it fun. Piper's not like the others. She's different. Fun. Sweet. Charming..." I trailed off and licked my lower lip. "Sexy as hell."

"And a klutz to boot," Allister pointed out with a grin. "Can you imagine her as a vampire? She'd try to bite someone and end up killing them because she tripped over her own fangs."

We laughed together and then grew quiet, each of us falling into our own thoughts. As I moved toward my bed, I went about gathering my phone charger and toiletries to pack in my bag. I had already grabbed my clothes for the trip, and Darren had put it in the car to go to the private airport. Since it was still day time, we had blacked-out windows for the car, well, limo, there were too many of us to drive a regular car. Plus, Antoine had a thing for limos.

I wondered if Piper has ever been in one.

The prospect of seeing her face when we got in the limo or even the private plane had my anger dwindling and me humming a happy song.

"What's made you so chipper?" Allister asked as he clapped me on the shoulder.

I lifted a shoulder and dropped it with a wink. "Just thought of something better to obsess about."

Chuckling, Allister shook my shoulders with an annoyingly vigorous force. "Ugh, if you weren't my twin, I'd murder you."

I shoved his hands off and threw my bag over my shoulder before pointing a finger at him. "Right back at you, bro."

We chuckled on our way upstairs where the others were waiting. Piper was nowhere to be seen, but Darren had the limo waiting in the garage so we wouldn't have to go into the sun and Antoine was already in it... or so he said.

"Where's Piper?" I asked, looking around for the adorable blonde as I climbed in the back of the car. I sat with my brother on the far side of the limo, Marcus to my left, and Wynn and Rayne to the right. Antoine had the back seat completely to himself. That didn't really bother me because he spent most of our rides staring at his phone like he was doing now.

Antoine didn't even look up from his phone as he said the most pretentious thing I'd ever heard. "She's up front with Darren, where she belongs."

"So, an hour ago, she was family, and now, she's back to being the hired help?" I growled, leaning forward in my seat as I refrained from throwing myself across the limo at him.

Antoine let out an impatient sigh and sat his phone down long enough to meet my gaze. "She is still an employee, Draconius. Being part of the family doesn't change that, and besides, if she were back here, you would all fight over her." He lifted his phone back up to tap something out. "She's much more comfortable up there with Darren and not you panting lot."

I snorted. We'll see about that. I turned in my seat and tapped on the darkened separator to the front seat. It slowly lowered to reveal a serious Darren and a cheerful Piper who was bouncing in her seat.

"Why, hello there, lovely." I grinned at her through the window. "Am I correct in assuming you've never been in a limo?"

Piper grinned at me and bobbed her head. "This is really cool. I always wanted to ride in a limo. I mean, some of the kids in high school rented them for prom, but I wasn't allowed to. My parents..." She trailed off and then shook her head with a smile. "Never mind. I'm just excited to be here."

I glanced at my brother and then back to her with a mischievous wink. "Well, you aren't really experiencing it up there."

Before she could protest, Allister and I reached over the seat and pulled her through the window. She landed in our laps, her lower half sprawled in Allister's lap and her upper half in mine. Piper giggled like a fiend and wiggled in place.

"Oh, don't do that, love. You'll wake the one-eyed snake."

Wynn made a pained sound.

"What's the one-eyed snake?" Piper blinked innocently up at me. I was thankful she had chosen to wear jeans today because I didn't think I could handle her in a skirt back here. The temptation was just too great.

Rayne scoffed and shoved a pair of headphones in his ears after saying, "He means his dick."

Piper's eyes widened, and she shifted out of my lap into Allister's. Allister grinned like the smug bastard he was as I threw my hands up in the air.

"Here I am, making sure you get the full limo experience, and this asshole gets the benefits from it." I shook my head in mock disgust.

Allister held Piper closer and grinned over her head. "Well, I am the more attractive twin."

Piper giggled in his lap, and I scoffed. "You can't be more attractive. We're identical, down to our dick size."

"Really?" Piper's voice raised a pitch, and her eyes darted from my lap to Allister's as if really trying to see through our pants.

I gave her a saucy wink and shifted up to a crouch in the limo. "Wanna see? I'll prove it. Come on, Al, whip it out."

The others groaned and shifted away from us. Piper, though, was staring hard at my hands which had gone to my belt. However, before I could unbutton my pants, Antoine spoke up.

"The first one to disrobe in here will be walking to the hangar naked."

I groaned in disappointment before buckling my belt and sitting back down with a huff.

Piper glanced worriedly over at Antoine and then back to us. "Won't that kill you though? The sun?"

I lifted a shoulder. "Not right away."

"Hurts like a bitch though," Rayne piped in, showing he was actually listening through his headphones.

Wynn even chimed in, "Excruciatingly painful."

Piper tensed in Allister's arms and chewed on her lower lip. I could tell she wanted to know more but was afraid to ask, so I went ahead and put her out of her misery.

"It depends on how old you are," I explained. "Like, Rayne here. He's the youngest of us, only a few decades old. He would probably make it to the hangar with just third-degree burns, nothing a little blood couldn't heal, but Antoine over there?" I pointed at the blonde aristocrat who was determined to pretend we didn't exist. "He is well over a few centuries old." Piper gasped as her eyes darted to Antoine's. She might not notice it, but I saw the way he puffed up his chest and tried to look more attractive to her eyes. "He would turn to dust in a matter of minutes."

Piper's shocked face showed a bit of awe and pity for our fearless leader. I had to admit that I was a bit jealous. I wanted her to look at me that way. Well, not the pity, but the rest of it? Totally.

When we arrived at the airport, we waited in the limo for a moment, not quite ready to get out and leave the cozy setting we'd created with all six of us. Eventually, we couldn't delay any longer. We filed out of the limo one at a time until it was just Piper, Allister, and me. I grabbed Piper's hand before she could leave and asked her a question that had been bothering me the whole way here.

"You're going to become bonded, aren't you?" I met her eyes with a bit of hesitancy, unsure of what she would say. We had all been saying, 'oh we're family, she's ours,' but she has yet to say what she wanted. Would Piper bind herself to us? Or would she rather take the risk?

The small smile that played on her lips made me sigh out the tension I was holding even before she murmured shyly, "Yes. I will."

CHAPTER 21
Piper

WHAT FOLLOWED AFTER STEPPING out of the limo and into the hangar was not what I expected. I'd been to the airport before, but to be in a private hangar about to board a private plane the masters owned was something else.

There was no checking the bags, no getting scanned for explosives or liquids, none of that stuff. I was even handed a glass of champagne as I stepped into the plane.

"I could get used to this," I murmured to myself as I took in the plane.

There were four chairs total with a couple of couch-like seats lining the sides of the cabin. A large television filled the back wall with a door on either side of it. I tried to see what was in it without acting too nosy but was greeted by two gorgeous stewardesses, dressed in black skirt suits with blood red neckties.

They both smiled and ushered me into the cabin. One of them told me to sit wherever I wanted while the other greeted the masters. I was too nervous to sit through.

I hadn't thought much about being bonded to them before. but as the time to see their sire grew closer, I realized that they very well meant to have me do it before we got there, maybe even here on the plane. My stomach rolled around at the thought of being bound to them.

Would it hurt? Would I still be me?

Darren was kind of a stick in the mud and did whatever they wanted without question. Had he always been that way, or would I become some kind of robot that would do whatever they needed?

A dark part of me shivered at the prospect of being their puppet, and I shook my head in disgust. Of course, my slutty ass would think about them fucking me and not about how they would own me. I sighed and searched for a seat.

"Breathe, Piper." Darren's voice preceded him as he appeared at my side so suddenly that I jumped in place.

I spun around to face him and gave him a weak smile before forcing myself to take a few deep breaths. With Darren here, I felt a bit better, not so much at my masters' mercy.

The masters came behind him, and I had to either move out of the way or get trampled. I sat in one of the cream leather seats. It had so much more leg room than a normal plane that I could curl up in the seat and fall asleep if I wanted to.

Wynn took the seat next to me, much to my delight. The others piled in behind him with Rayne giving me a disheartened frown before taking a seat across from us with Marcus. The twins sat behind us while Antoine took a seat by himself, already pulling the tray table open to type away on a laptop he brought. Darren was up front, talking to the pilot and stewardesses about the plans for the flight.

I turned my attention back to the vampire next to me. Wynn seemed perfectly at ease and not at all nervous about the ride. He leaned on the arm of his chair and peered at me through half-lidded eyes.

"So, are you excited?"

"I'm not sure." I shrugged. "It depends on what you're referring to."

"The plane ride, of course." Wynn blinked those long lashes at me with a sultry smile. "None of us are excited about seeing our sire.

"Where are we going again?" I shifted in my seat and fiddled with the different buttons on my seat. When one of them made the seat fall back into a reclining position, I let out a little gasp of shock.

Allister peered over my seat with an amused grin. "Why, hello there."

I giggled and pushed the button again to make my seat move up right again. Wynn watched me with growing amusement, his face laying on his hand.

"To answer your question," he said, "we are going to Seattle."

"Washington?" My brows shot up to my hairline. I was shocked by how far away their sire lived.

"Yep," Drake popped as he leaned between our seats. "We wanted to get as far away from him as possible without leaving the country."

"Because he would never allow that," Wynn added, his voice full of disdain. "I'd have loved to see Paris again. It's my home city, you know?"

"You're French?" My mouth dropped open slightly. "I couldn't tell. You don't have much of an accent."

Wynn's eyes crinkled at the edges. "Why, thank you." He picked my hand up and lifted it to his mouth before spouting out something lovely and very decidedly French that I didn't understand but made heat pool in between my thighs.

"What'd you say?" I breathed, ignoring the fact that every one of them had stopped talking to inhale my scent. I really needed to get a handle on that. I couldn't so much as fart in this more-than-spacious plane, let alone get turned on.

Rayne snorted from his seat and leaned to one side, meeting my eyes over Marcus's large frame. "Don't be so impressed. He simply said it's easy to fool the idiot Americans."

Wynn gave Rayne a venomous glare before turning back to me. "I also said that it is an honor for such a great beauty to compliment me so."

"That's sweet." I flushed but still punched him in the arm. "Say something else."

For the next half-hour, Wynn talked to me in French which only made the twins jealous, so they started to wow me with their German and Russian. I'd never been very good at languages, but hearing these gorgeous men speaking to me in exotic, foreign tongues made my insides flip over with pleasure.

"If you're done with the language lesson," Rayne drawled with much annoyance, "we only have a few hours before we land, and we still have something rather important to deal with." He leveled a meaningful look around the cabin, and I stiffened.

The bonding. Crap, I'd forgotten all about that. Shifting forward in my seat, I twisted my hair around my fingers.

"So, what do I have to do?" My voice came out small and shaky, my fear for what was to come peeking through.

Darren appeared next to our row. "Drink some more of this," He shoved another champagne flute into my hands, "and decide who will be the one to do it."

I took the alcohol and downed it in one go before croaking out, "What? Pick who?"

Darren leveled a stare at me. "Who will be the one to bind you to them."

I gaped at him as the others stared at me. I could feel their eyes pushing against my skin as they waited for me to answer.

"But, but I thought it was going to be something like a group thing?" When they didn't answer back right away, I quickly added, "Like a general binding, not like I have to pick one of you to be bound to forever. And why does it have to be forever? Can't it just be for like this weekend?" I found myself talking even faster as my panic set in. "Maybe just a little binding? Not the whole shebang?" Now I was gesturing rapidly with my hands, and I desperately wanted another glass of champagne to help deal with it all.

"No, you can't just kind of be bound," Rayne scoffed. It has to be all or nothing. Do you want Valentine to steal you away? Because he will at the first opportunity, and when he binds you to him, it won't be consensual or pleasant. At least with us, you get to choose and at least have some kind of freedom."

My shoulders sagged at that. "So, I won't be some mindless zombie doing whatever you want?"

Wynn smirked and gave me a suggestive look. "Only if you want to be."

Normally, I would have blushed and flirted back, but I was too full of fear and anxiety to even become aroused. My body was on full alert and not in a nice way. I licked my lips and swallowed thickly.

"So, what does being bound mean? Will you have power over me? Will I have to drink blood?" Just saying it made me sick to my stomach, and I had to hold back the urge to puke up all the alcohol I'd just drank.

"Not at all." Drake shifted to between our chairs so he could meet my eyes. "In some ways, you'll actually be immune to a lot of our abilities. Plus, you'll live longer, you won't get sick."

"Oh, and you'll have heightened senses," Allister added from behind me. "I mean, like all your senses."

"What he means is don't be weirded out if you are abnormally turned on by whoever you're bound to. It's part of the process," Rayne jumped in again, being the blunt one of the group which at that moment I appreciated. I didn't want it watered down. I wanted to know what I was getting into.

I nodded numbly and stared off at the wall. I didn't know how to respond to all this or even how to begin to pick one of them. Thankfully, the stewardess came over and asked us all to buckle up because we were about to take off.

I took the time it took us to lift up into the sky and level out to think about it. The take-off, by the way, was so much easier than a regular plane. I hardly noticed the difference at all, and it was so much quieter. I could actually hear myself think which, at the moment, was a good and bad thing.

After the nice stewardess let us know we could unbuckle, I darted up from my chair and headed for the back of the plane where I knew one of the doors had to lead to a bathroom. The first one I tried on the left didn't. It opened up to a queen-sized bed fully equipped with pillows and blankets. It was just as nice as the one I had at home. Why they needed a bed on the plane was beyond me, but I didn't have time to worry about it right now. My bladder was ready to burst from all the champagne I'd drunk, and my head was swimming with it.

I rushed to the other door and sighed as I found a full bathroom including a shower and a sink. No tiny toilet closet that you had to somehow get in and do your business without getting it everywhere.

As I did my business, I tried to figure out who was going to do it. Who would I want to be bound to for all eternity? Fucking no one really, but I didn't have much of a choice. It was either do this or be at Valentine's mercy.

So, who to do it with?

Not Marcus. He was a nice enough guy, but I didn't know him well enough to get that close with him. Plus, I still wasn't sure he really liked me much.

The twins were a no-go as well. I just knew that being bound to one of them would cause a rift between them. I couldn't do that to them.

Wynn would be the obvious choice to most. I was attracted to him already, and I'd already taken his blood before, so I kind of knew what to expect. However, he was a massive flirt, and I wasn't sure he wouldn't screw me over with his playboy ways.

That just left Rayne and Antoine.

I washed my hands in the sink and chewed over the choice. I liked Rayne, even if he put his foot in his own mouth half the time. Also, we were kind of on our way to something, a relationship, maybe? I didn't know, but I did know that being bound to him would make all of that even more confusing.

With a sigh, I realized there really was only one choice. I should have seen it before. Antoine was the head of the house. He had more pull over what went on, and Valentine seemed a bit afraid of him which was a huge plus for me. Also, while we were attracted to one another, he seemed to be into Darren too. I wasn't sure if that was because of their bond or not, but Darren seemed okay with it so it couldn't be all that bad.

I paused right before the bathroom door, my hand on the knob. I hated to make this choice. I knew it would hurt Rayne as well as the others. I just hoped they would understand my choice and respect it.

If not, I was destroying any chance I had with them.

CHAPTER 22
Piper

WALKING BACK INTO THAT cabin was like walking into the gauntlet. I knew they were all going to be waiting for my answer, and I was dreading every second I came closer to having to tell them.

"Miss Billings?" Darren stepped out from his seat and approached me. The poker face he usually wore softened to let his concern peek through. "Piper?"

I swallowed, let out a shaky breath, then nodded to him. "I'm alright. I've decided."

The masters stood from their seats, all of them looking in my direction. Well, all but Antoine. He was still typing on his computer without a care or even an inkling that I would be picking him. I tried not to look at him so the others wouldn't guess before I could get it out.

I knew when Rayne read my mind. He let out a curse, and his amber eyes met mine briefly. They were so filled with disappointment and pain that I wanted to run to his side and console him, but I had made my decision. I couldn't back out now, not because I didn't want to hurt his feelings or the others. This wasn't about us. This was about making sure Valentine stayed away.

So, when Rayne gave me a curt nod, I offered him an apologetic shrug before turning to the rest of them. As I laced my fingers in front of me, I grappled for my words.

"I know this is a big decision, and I don't want any of you to think I didn't think this over. I did. I also want to make sure you all know that just because I have chosen someone else, that doesn't mean that I feel any differently about any of you. I chose the one I did because he was the right person for the job, the person I felt would be the biggest deterrent to Valentine and cause the least amount of fighting among you."

"Ah, fuck," Drake groaned as he slammed his open palm to his forehead. "You choose that asshole." He jerked his head toward Antoine with a grimace.

Antoine still hadn't stood or even shown any indication he was listening, but I nodded. "Yes, I choose Antoine."

There was a collective moan of protests from the others save for Marcus who simply watched with those dark eyes of his. I had a feeling he didn't much care one way or the other. That was good, it meant one less person's feelings I had to worry about.

"Now, I don't want you to think that I'm picking him over any of you." I paused and moved closer to Antoine in hopes of grabbing his attention. "He's the head of your house, and as well as being the oldest, Valentine already showed he hated him at the dinner party."

"Pfft." Allister shook his head. "Valentine hates all of us. If that's what you're basing it on—"

"I'm not." I shook my head as I interrupted him. "I mean, I'm not just basing it on that. Antoine's also already bound someone before, well, unless you have some human servants hiding under your bed?" I scrambled to add, trying to make them understand. When I glanced around the cabin, and they all shook their heads, I relaxed slightly. "I didn't think so."

"But Piper..." Wynn approached me, his hand grabbing mine and drawing them to his chest. "I don't think you know what you're getting into. Antoine won't only be bound to you by blood, but he'll be able to feel your emotions, find you no matter where you are."

I swallowed and nodded dumbly. "I understand, but Antoine is the only one who hasn't tried to seduce me. Sure, he's used my attraction for him to get me to do what he wanted, but not the way the rest of you have." I licked my lips and shot a look his way, expecting him to speak up, but he simply watched me speak with an unreadable expression.

Rayne snorted. "So, you're picking him because he wouldn't give you the time of day? What a womanly thing to do."

I glared at the redhead. "That's not what I said at all."

"No, no, we get it." Rayne held his hands up with a growl. "He won't get emotional about it is what you're saying."

"Something like that," I tried to explain further, but Rayne jumped in again.

"Then you might as well have had Marcus do it. As far as ice sculptures go, he's about as frigid as they come." Rayne gestured to the large stoic man who simple glowered down at him.

I opened my mouth to argue further why I hadn't chosen Marcus when Antoine finally spoke up.

"Enough. Piper has made her decision." He stood and buttoned his suit jacket before meeting me in the middle of the aisle. "We only have a short time before we land. If you still have protests, save them for afterward, or better yet, wait until we are back home where they can't be used against us." His eyes moved around the cabin, making each of the brothers shrink back into their seats.

See? That was exactly the reason I picked him. All he had to do was look around the room, and they stopped their arguing. If my being bound to one of them was going to stop Valentine, then Antoine was the one to do it.

The vampire in question brushed past me and walked to the door on the left, the one with the queen-sized bed in it. I wondered at the implication but didn't question it. I didn't want to do this in front of everyone anyway. The fewer people watching, the better.

I glanced around at the others for one brief second before making my way to the back. Darren stood by the doorway waiting for me. I paused before him and then had to ask, "Is it worth it?"

Darren reached up and patted the side of my face with his white-gloved hand and gave me a reassuring look. "Yes. A hundred times, yes."

I let out a long-relieved breath. "Stay with me?"

This time he shook his head. "This isn't something you share with another. Don't worry, Master Durand was the right choice." With those parting words, he left me at the doorway and took his seat once more.

I watched him go, then took a shaky breath, turning back to the bedroom. Antoine sat on a chair off to one side, watching me as if he had all the time in the world. I fidgeted with my hands, lacing them together before releasing them to swing my arms back and forth.

"So, uh, how do we do this?"

"Shut the door."

My brows raised before I clamped my mouth shut and did as he asked. "Of course, sure. That makes sense. Wouldn't want anyone staring at us, huh?"

I let out a nervous laugh and wrapped my arms around my waist as I waited by the now-closed door for Antoine to give me some kind of direction.

"Piper." My head jerked up to meet his pale eyes. "Calm yourself. You're hyping this up too much in your head."

"Oh." I let out a small laugh, feeling really silly. "Sorry. I just don't know what to expect."

Antoine stopped me with a raised hand. "You chose me for a reason, one you were quite forthcoming in letting us all. So, now I'm going to be the same as you and be utterly forthright." He paused as he stood and approached me with a predatory look in his eyes. "Blood binding is not something you do just for protection. Most don't do it at all unless they are... emotionally attached." Antoine gave me a meaningful look until I made a sort of o-face.

"Oh, okay. I got it. Like lovers or whatever." I waved a hand, my heart jumping further into my throat the closer he got to me.

"Yes, precisely." His words grew low as his eyelids dipped down. For a second, I thought his eyes moved to my lips before they were back on my face. "So, the process isn't exactly appealing."

"What do you mean?" My head cocked to the side, my already frazzled nerves becoming even more entangled.

"It's painful," he bluntly explained, his eyes focused on my reaction. "I believe one once described it as having fire running through their veins. Ironically, that is similar to how it feels when to be turned into a vampire."

"Oh."

"So, you see why it is usually lovers who do this kind of thing." He inclined his head toward me as if he were trying to get some point across that I wasn't catching.

"Because it isn't worth the pain?" I arched a brow as my feet swiveled from side to side.

Antoine smirked and leaned in even closer. "Because most of them do the blood exchange while fucking."

I gasped and pulled back, my face burning from hearing those words come from his accented mouth. "Wha... what? You want us to... you and I to have sex?"

Antoine shrugged an elegant shoulder and turned his head to the side. "Unless you prefer to be in unbearable pain?"

"No, no." I shook my head rapidly and swallowed hard. I did not handle pain well, not at all. I whined when I pulled a tangle out of my hair. However, having sex with Antoine hadn't been what I'd signed up for when I chose him to bind me.

Antoine seemed to see my struggle, stepped back, and gestured toward the door. "If it would make you more comfortable, we can have one of the others do the actual act, and I will just do the binding."

"One of the others?" I couldn't believe he was actually suggesting what I thought he was suggesting.

Antoine tucked his hands into his pockets, pushing his suit jack back as if he hadn't just asked one of his brothers to join us in the bedroom. "Perhaps Wynn or Rayne? Which one are you into right now?"

The shock in my system quickly cooled at his question. I scowled. "I'm not some flighty woman who is jumping back and forth between them. I like them both. I mean, all of them." I huffed and planted my hands on my hips. "Besides, it's not like they aren't coming on to me. You've done it too."

Antoine gave me a wicked grin. "But didn't you just say I only try to seduce you when I want something?"

I gaped at him as anger slipped away to shock. "So, you were listening?"

"Fervently."

I winced and brushed a hair behind my ear. "Look, I stand by what I said. I think you're the right choice, but..." I sighed and dropped my arms beside me. "I'm not particularly into pain, and while having sex with you might not be what I had signed up for, I don't think it would be the worst thing in the world."

"Why, thank you, I'm glad I'm not so repulsive for you."

Cringing at the bite in his voice, I tried to correct myself. "That's not what I meant. I mean, I just didn't expect to be having sex with my boss."

"You won't be." Antoine removed his jacket and folded it over the arm of the nearby chair. His hands went to his tie where he loosened it but didn't remove it. He rolled his sleeves up, and I'd never been so intrigued by someone's biceps before.

"What are you doing?" I gaped, my voice already becoming husky.

Antoine offered me a knowing grin before taking a seat on the edge of the bed. "Things may become a bit messy, and I don't want to ruin my best suit."

I snorted. "I've seen your closet, that's hardly your best suit, or even your only suit. You have nothing but suits."

"Have you been snooping, Miss Billings?" Antoine said with an arched brow, his eyes twinkling with amusement.

I tossed my hair over my shoulder and then crossed my arms over my chest with a scoff. "Uh, no. I do the laundry, duh."

"But not my suits. Those are done by Darren who gets them dry cleaned. So, the only reason you have to be in my closet is to snoop."

I stared him down, refusing to budge and admit that he was right. I had been snooping. Who wouldn't? I mean, I lived in a house with six hot vampires. Of course, I was going to snoop. I had to, or I'd go insane.

Antoine's lips ticked at the side before he quirked a finger at me. "Come here."

Still not sure he had given up on it, I shifted in place. Then after giving myself a little pep talk, I dropped my arms and walked toward him. I stopped at the edge of the bed not sure if I should sit, stand, or take my clothes off?

"Have a seat," Antoine commanded in that deliciously demanding tone of his.

I sat down promptly and pressed my legs together tightly, my eyes falling to my lap where my hands were curled into fists. This was so weird. I'd never been in this sort of position. When I planned on having sex with a guy, it was spontaneous. We'd start with some kissing and then make our way to sex. Antoine was staring at me like I was supposed to lay back and spread my legs for him.

"Piper, this is about you, not me. Take your pleasure to wash away the pain." Antoine's voice turned low and sultry. That seductive sound mixed with the words themselves to instantly make my body warm, and I squirmed in place. Seriously, it would give Wynn a run for his money.

Antoine's finger placed under my chin and tipped my head back. My eyelashes fluttered as I lifted them to see the desire on his usually professional face. My tongue wet my lower lip and brushed against Antoine's thumb at the same time. I immediately withdrew my tongue and swallowed, my mouth dropping open slightly as the tension between us became thick.

"I'm going to kiss you," Antoine told me moments before his mouth descended on mine. My hands went to his shirt, clenching around the fabric of his shirt as I held him close to me.

Antoine's kiss was demanding just like the man himself. He didn't ask permission to deepen the kiss, he nipped at my lip instead, causing me to gasp and open my mouth to him. He plundered my mouth and wrapped his hands around my waist as he leaned me back on the bed.

I let loose a surprised moan as I found myself on my back with him perched between my thighs. One of my legs was thrown over his hip, and he ground his erection against my core. I let out small whimpering sounds of need as the heat built. I ached for us to take it further but too embarrassed by the whole situation to do anything but let him take control.

That was something Antoine didn't have any problem doing. He pulled my tongue far enough into his mouth that his fangs nicked one side, making me hiss, but he was quick to sooth the pain by sucking on the wound. Now it was his turn to moan and grind against me.

His hand moved up my hip and under my shirt, groping for my breast through my bra. I ached, hot for more. I wanted him to strip me bare and burrow inside of me while his fangs plunged into my neck.

Wow, where did that come from? I'd never wanted someone to bite me so badly.

I pulled my mouth away from him and took in deep breaths. My fingers let go of his shirt and fumbled with the buttons, but I just wasn't able to get my hands to work right. Antoine smirked and shifted back to unbutton his shirt slowly, his eyes moving over my face, past my swollen lips and down to my puckered nipples. His nostrils flared as he inhaled deeply, no doubt smelling my arousal in the air.

Crap. If he could smell it then the others... My eyes moved to the door, briefly wondering if they could hear me. Oh, God. What was I going to say to them? I mean, I already had confirmation about the sharing, but I'd never asked Antoine about it.

"Stop thinking, Piper," Antoine demanded, his shirt already off his shoulders. My eyes locked onto the muscular form he'd unwrapped for me. Without thinking, my fingers moved up to the sigil tattooed into his skin. I traced the letters and picture, watching as Antoine's breath came in small pants.

Interesting.

My gaze moved from his chest to his eyes, and I chewed on my lower lip before sitting up. I grabbed the bottom of my shirt and pulled it over my head. I did as he bid and stopped thinking as I unsnapped my bra and laid bare myself before him.

I could feel Antoine's hot gaze move over my skin, making me squirm beneath him. With a smug smirk, Antoine shifted lower and brushed his fingers against my hip bone without asking, which seemed his go-to, but hey, I already said yes. How we got there didn't really matter that much.

When Antoine's fingers found my soaked folds, I gasped and closed my eyes, no longer able to keep my thoughts straight. While his one hand was busy, he dragged down the rest of my clothing, leaving me naked and aching for him.

As he dragged out each and every moan and small cry of pleasure, I was astutely aware of his movements. How he was able to juggle torturing me while pulling the rest of his clothing off, I had no idea, but I thanked whatever god or demon for it as I came apart on his hand.

Gasping from my release, I looked up at him from beneath heavy lids. Antoine removed his hand and shifted into place so that he cupped the back of my neck and brought me up to meet his kiss. He shifted me into his lap and sank me down onto his long hard length while his mouth took control of my breath. I could do nothing but hold onto for dear life.

Oh, God. I couldn't. It was too much. I couldn't breathe. I needed... I needed...

Antoine released my mouth and reared back before sinking his fangs into my neck. Pain burst from where he bit me, and I squealed, scrambling to get away. Antoine held onto me tightly and tilted his hips so that he hit somewhere inside of me. The intense pleasure had my eyes rolling back in my head, the pain in my neck no more than an itch. To add injury to my already scrambled mind, Antoine somehow got his hand in between us and punched down on my clit, making me break apart at the seams.

While I orgasmed, I felt something happen. Something rushed through me, lighting my body and veins on fire but not so much that it took away from the pleasure I felt. I firmly understood why only lovers did this. It was quite a ride.

Just as I thought I couldn't get enough, Antoine released my neck and bit into his wrist. His bleeding wound was pressed against my mouth, and I parted my lips without question. If I thought I'd tasted blood before, I'd never tasted a vampire's blood like this before. I couldn't describe how it tasted, but it was like drinking down sunshine and power.

It was so heady that Antoine had to pull me away just to get me to stop. I let out a groan of protest, but then my eyes grew heavy. He laid me back on the bed and pulled the cover up over me. A soft hand brushed the hair away from my face, and Antoine's lips caressed my forehead before darkness overtook me.

CHAPTER 23
Antoine

LEAVING PIPER IN THE bedroom by herself was one of the hardest things I had ever done. With Darren's binding, I had stayed by his side until he awoke, but it was different with her. It wasn't just me who wanted her affection, so I couldn't be selfish with her.

"Where's Piper?" Drake asked as he stood from his chair, looking around as if I was hiding her behind me. "Is she alright?"

I glanced down at the cuffs of my suit jacket and adjusted them. "She's alive and well. She's sleeping now."

"And you just left her there by herself?" Rayne snarled at me, jumping out of his chair to bound down the aisle.

I released an impatient breath and tucked my hands into my pockets as I stared the redhead down. "She will be fine. Darren is in there with her."

This didn't satisfy Rayne. His eyes flashed red, and he moved dangerously close to me. "But you're the one who is bound to her. You just fucked her, and now, you're going to pretend like nothing happened?"

"Yes, I am," I spoke firmly without giving anything away to the rest of them.

"You're an ass," Rayne snapped and flashed his fangs at me.

I let out a weary sigh. "If you're so worried about her, why don't you go wait for her to wake up? I have business to attend to."

Rayne's mouth clamped shut, and he mustered up a glare. "Maybe I will, since you don't give two licks about her." He shoved past me and stalked into the bedroom.

A few seconds later, Darren left the room and came to me, his eyes watching me curiously. Not wanting my longtime companion to see what I hid from my brothers, I slipped back into my seat and pulled open my laptop.

In most situations, had Rayne defied me in such a way, I would have put him in his place, reminded him who was in charge, and who exactly he owed his life to... but not this time. Not when I knew that the only reason he was acting this way was because of her.

Piper had wiggled her way not just into our home, but into each and every one of our hearts, whether she knew it or not. While our attraction to her was permeable, how each of us felt about her individually was another matter. It made each of us do things we wouldn't normally do, and one of those was putting her best interest in the place of our own.

I was no good for her. I might be the one she chose to bind her, but I also knew there was a reason for it that was not love. No, Piper chose me because I was safe. Sure, we teased and flirted with one another, but I was her boss. In her mind, I was the only boss regardless of what part my brothers played in it all.

There was a moment while I was in her mind, our bodies joined physically, mentally, and biologically, that I knew in perfect clarity the reason she chose me. She couldn't see herself falling for me... ever.

So, I had to give her what she wanted, regardless of how much it pained me to do so. I could feel her in my chest even now, a heat that was so much more than what I had ever felt Darren. Even in her sleep, she was a light in the darkness, causing turmoil in my long-deadened heart.

While I pretended to check my emails, I could feel eyes on me. I tried to shake them off, but they were persistent in their glare. As I sighed with much annoyance, I glanced up from my laptop to meet Wynn's gaze.

"What is it now?"

Wynn moved from his seat to the empty one next to me. "Tell me, did you know you would have to have sex with her when she announced that she'd chose you?"

"I knew it was a possibility," I retorted truthfully before looking back at my computer. A second later, the screen slapped shut with a snap. I looked up and found Wynn a foot away with more emotion in his eyes than I'd seen in a long time.

"Did you enjoy it? Or was it just another necessary evil?" Wynn hissed and leaned forward so that the hand on my laptop creaked.

I leaned back in my seat and stared at him. As I laced my hands in my lap, I chose my words carefully, a hint of a smirk on my lips. "Oh, I enjoyed her... thoroughly."

Wynn growled, and my laptop creaked more.

Narrowing my eyes on him, I reached out and grabbed his wrist. "Break my laptop, and I'll make sure she never so much as sniffs in your direction again."

"You don't have the power to do that," Wynn countered, but there was a hint of doubt in his eyes. He wasn't a hundred percent sure about that.

Good.

I threw his hand away and leaned forward to meet his gaze. "You don't know what all I'm capable of, brother, but I hope you remember before we arrive at our sire's home. While Valentine might be a pest, our sire is no puppy. We'll need every ounce of strength we can get, and if that means I have to fuck our lovely Piper again right in front of everyone, I will do so."

The twins, who had been quiet during this altercation, made resounding sounds of disapproval, but I ignored them, focusing on Wynn.

"I will not let all our hard work go to ruin. The House of Durand will stand, or so help me God, I will see it all burn to ash."

With those words, Wynn left, going back to his seat and leaving me in a false peace. I opened my computer back up, but I didn't have the energy to even pretend to be working. Instead, I leaned my head back and closed my eyes.

Behind my lids was the memory of Piper. Her face as she cried out for me. The brush of her lips against mine. The taste of her on my tongue. It wasn't something I would easily forget any time soon, no matter how much I wanted to.

My eyes weren't closed long when the back door opened. Even through my eyelids, I could see her, feel her, a beacon of light that moved through the plane and came so close that I could touch her, but I refrained.

Piper's presence stopped at the end of my aisle. I could feel her hesitance, the insecurity rushing through her. Still, I kept my eyes closed. The disappointment and confusion that filled her almost made me give in, but I didn't. If anyone were paying attention to me, they'd see my hands tightening on the armrests of my chair.

I waited until she moved further down the aisle and sat next to Wynn before opening my eyes to slits, just enough to see the top of her head in her chair. I ached to see more, but then my view was obstructed by Darren, staring down at me with disapproval and pity.

I snapped my eyes to the side, giving up the gig that I was sleeping. Without asking permission, Darren took the seat next to me and just sat there. He didn't say anything the rest of the plane ride, even as my brother Wynn consoled Piper by calling me all manner of names. Darren was just there for me like he always has been, and I knew always would.

"Please put your seats back to an upright position. We will be landing shortly," the stewardess announced before walking the length of the plane to make landing preparations.

Seattle, Washington was cold and rainy. They had more dark days than sunny ones. That fact along made it the perfect home for one of the largest vampire nests in the United States. I didn't particularly care for the weather, being wet had never been something I enjoyed, but the obscured sun allowed us to walk off the plane and into the afternoon air without the worry of being burned to a crisp. There was enough cloud cover that we could walk through the open airfield and then into the limo waiting for us.

This time Piper didn't sit in the front seat. She climbed into the back, giving me a curious look before she took the seat next to Rayne. He took her hand and wrapped an arm around her shoulders.

Jealousy flared inside of me, but I pushed it down, happy that our bond of emotions was only one way. I needed to be able to put on the mask that I hadn't worn in years, and I couldn't do that if Piper kept getting in the way.

No, she'd have to wait until we were safe to get her answers. I hadn't been lying when I said I wouldn't let anything jeopardize our house. Not even her. Not even me.

"Master Durand," Darren lowered the window between us and glanced back from the passenger seat a few moments later, "we've arrived."

Piper's heartbeat jumped in her chest, and she twisted in her seat to stare out the window at the expansive mansion. I didn't need to see it to know what she saw. I used to live here, and it was all the same, even after all these years. It was a gorgeous landscape with awe-inspiring architecture meant to put you at ease before you realized that the spider's lair was real, and you just walked into its web.

I adjusted my suit jacket and scanned the limo. As I put my best authoritative tone in my voice, I asked, "Well, brothers, are you ready for this?"

ABOUT THE AUTHOR

Erin Bedford is an otaku, recovering coffee addict, and Legend of Zelda fanatic. Her brain is so full of stories that need to be told that she must get them out or explode into a million screaming chibis. Obsessed with fairy tales and bad boys, she hasn't found a story she can't twist to match her deviant mind full of innuendos, snarky humor, and dream guys.

On the outside, she's a work from home mom and bookbinger. One the inside, she's a thirteen-year-old boy screaming to get out and tell you the pervy joke they found online. As an ex-computer programmer, she dreams of one day combining her love for writing and college credits to make the ultimate video game!

Until then, when she's not writing, Erin is devouring as many books as possible on her quest to have the biggest book gut of all time. She's written over thirty books, ranging from paranormal romance, urban fantasy, and even scifi romance.

Come chat me up!
www.erinbedford.com
Facebook.com/erinbedfordauthor
Instagram.com/erinbedfordauthor
twitter.com/erin_bedford
tiktok.com/@erinbedfordauthor

www.ingramcontent.com/pod-product-compliance
Lightning Source LLC
Chambersburg PA
CBHW071737190726
48292CB00003B/780